# BUGGED

## & OTHER STORIES

**Also by Amandine Guise**

DALNEUCH, DECEASED – a novel
An Clò Beag Glas, 2019

In preparation:
THE STAGE WE'RE AT – a novel
An Clò Beag Glas, 2021

# BUGGED
## & OTHER STORIES

**TWENTY-FIVE SHORT STORIES BY**

## AMANDINE GUISE

with 33 illustrations by
**EGIDIA NEUSMAN**

First published 2020 by An Clò Beag Glas, Lochcarron, IV54 8YB

ISBN 978-0-9539057-9-9

Illustrations © Egidia Neusman

British Library Cataloguing-in Publication Data

A catalogue record for this book is available from The British Library

Text set in 10.5pt Baskerville

Book design by D•iv•G, Strasbourg

Printed & bound by Inky Little Fingers at www.inkylittlefingers.co.uk

## AMANDINE GUISE

was born in the northern French département of Alsace. Her mother was Scottish and her father French. She studied in Paris at both the Collège de France with Jerzy Grotowski and at the École Normale Supérieure where she attended courses by Samuel Beckett. Her late husband was a Scot. For many years a caravan on Skye was her frequent refuge until rampant and destructive tourism forced her to find somewhere quieter on the mainland in Wester Ross. It is here that she, until recently, had been expecting to remain but now fears that "Brexit" may make it impossible. In her younger days she was a vintage car devotee and member of two dedicated French clubs; examples of many of the vehicles she owned, but which sat mainly on her study mantlepiece, may be found in her work.


## EGIDIA NEUSMAN

is a painter, print-maker and illustrator who, since childhood, has been a staunch friend & ally of author Amandine Guise with whom she shares a history not entirely dissimilar She has studied and worked in nine European art institutes. Her professional career began in architecture and design, later expanding to encompass scenography; her printmaking and painting has been exhibited from Sao Paulo to Moscow. Illustration is a relatively recent calling.

# CONTENTS

# LIST OF ILLUSTRATIONS

# INTRODUCTION

In the Table of Contents on page *vii* it will be seen that certain of the stories listed are marked by an asterisk.  The reason is this: those particular stories were written to be shared with the members of the writing group to which I belong here in the West Highland village that is my home.  The group meets perhaps ten times yearly to read out short stories and poems written in response to agreed titles.  I find this a stimulating exercise in itself;  but it also reminds me of the importance of words' sounds.  Words that can look very well on the page may prove to be elocutionary minefields – not in themselves so much as in the ways they are assembled.  Playwrights understand this; so too, do some poets; but it is not something to which the writers of prose often attend.  This was brought home to me many years ago when reading aloud to my young daughter the works of a well-known and highly-regarded children's author.  The stories were good; the characters strong; and the sentences all too often awkward or even ugly to say.  Read silently, there was no problem; but to speak them aloud was a very different matter. The author had only *seen* what he had written; he had not *heard* it. Not only did it lack euphony, it was tricky to articulate.  It was criss-crossed with phonetic tripwires.

So, given that more than half of the stories in this collection were written in order to be heard as much as to be read, I hope I have managed to avoid the pitfalls outlined above.

*That notorious Martyrdom of St Leodegar*

# I

# BUGGED

'I take it you've you heard?'

'Heard what?'

'About the confessionals!'

'What about the confessionals?'

'It seems there were hidden microphones!'

'Hidden microphones?  In the confessionals?  You mean they're bugged?'

'Well, of course, that's another matter entirely.  I voiced my doubts about Sister Veronica's thoroughness after that infestation of cockchafers in the choir'.

'I thought you were talking about secret microphones?'

'Was I?  Oh yes:  in the confessionals'.

'What, both of them?'

'That's what I was told'.

'By whom?'

'Mr Scrope.  And, as you know, there's no-one…'

'Quite.  But I think you said that there *were* hidden microphones?  May I assume that there are no longer any hidden microphones?'

'Mr Scrope didn't say; but I'm sure he used the past tense. And if Mr Scrope …'

'Quite.  Did…' (and here Lady Pamela looked more than a little concerned and raised an elegantly gloved hand to her mouth).  'Did you get any impression of just how long these … microphones … had been …concealed?'

'Mr Scrope seemed to think they'd been there quite some time:  he said the wires were quite dusty.  I blame Sister Veronica'.

'What?  Do you mean you think that Sister Veronica planted the microphones?'

'No, no:  I meant for the dust.  As I was saying a moment or two ago, I've had doubts about her thoroughness and this surely proves it'.

'I assume Fr Coughlin has been told?'

'It was Fr Coughlin himself found the microphones'.

'What?  How odd!  Is Fr Coughlin in the habit of searching the confessionals?'

'I wouldn't think so, not for one moment.  After all, we've Mr Scrope…'.

'Quite.    So why in heaven's name <u>was</u> Fr Coughlin searching the confessionals?'

'Mr Scrope wasn't too clear about that.    It appears Fr Coughlin said he was looking for a snap he'd mislaid.  But when Mr Scrope had asked Fr Coughlin about the snap and if he could help look for it, Fr Coughlin had become confused and said that what he'd said  was "scrap" – meaning a scrap of paper – and that, in any case, he'd found it.     But he did urge Mr Scrope to investigate the microphones – discretely'.  Mrs Warde-Bax paused and peered cautiously about her.    Bewdley's was unnaturally quiet for that time in the morning.  Consequently, as she realised, there was more chance than usual of being overheard.    She lowered both her head and her voice and breathed  'So he did'.

'Did what?'    Lady Pamela's curt question ricocheted off the terrazzo tiles, the marble-topped tables and the stained-glass windows.   Several yards away a man in dark tweeds dropped his newspaper to look, startled, across the intervening no-man's land and a black-clad waitress momentarily headed their way.  'What was it Mr Scrope did?' Lady Pamela murmured, more confidentially.

'Investigated the microphones.   It seems that somehow they were incorporated into those crucifixes over the grilles and the wires disappeared up through the roofs of the confessionals'.

'And then where did they go?'

'Behind that tapestry of St Leodegar at first – but after that it's a mystery'.

'Why? Didn't Mr Scrope follow them to see where they led?'

'No, he couldn't. He pulled them and got yards of wire and then two little plugs – I think he called them "jacks" – but couldn't work out where they had come from. It's such a large tapestry and who knows what's behind it'.

Lady Pamela remembered all too clearly what was behind that tapestry, that notorious *Martyrdom of St Leodegar* – what lay behind it both in respect of its physical position and its provenance. She recollected very well the scrofulous wall in the west transept, unaccountably robbed of the memorials with which it had once been covered and in which former openings had been but crudely blocked; the two, ornate, wooden confessionals had done little to hide the depredation and decay. She recollected the bishop's delight when her late mother-in-law proposed the commissioning of a huge tapestry for the afflicted area, to be executed as part of her will – though, tactfully, the bishop had hoped it would be many years before the work could be started. In the event, the Dowager Countess of Mountcashell met with a fatal accident at the Doncaster racecourse barely two years later and consequently the tapestry project was started somewhat earlier than might have been anticipated – and was then some twenty years in the making, both on account of its size and also the limitations of its weavers, all of whom were pupils at a nearby school for the blind. Meanwhile the bishop had been promoted, for undisclosed reasons, to the rank of archbishop *ad personam* and quietly retired into ecclesiastic obscurity; but his successor found himself inexorably constrained to continue the tapestry project. At its eventual unveiling, its reception had been mixed: Vladimir Petroslav writing in *The Guardian* describing it as "a fitting reflection on the need for timeous muscularity in contemporary Christian iconography"; Regan O'Renal, also in *The Guardian*, noted that the finished work bore little resemblance to the very early sketch by Mercia Tyne upon which it was based, but could not decide whether that in itself was either a good or a bad thing; while Byron Crewell, in the *Evening Standard*, thought it a blessing that its weavers could not see what they had done and a curse that everyone else could. The forcible optical exenteration, as he put it, of the unfortunate St Leodegar didn't bear looking at. But as a will was a will and a pious bequest a pious bequest: a vast tapestry of both textual and textural extremes had come to disguise both the disfigured masonry and the wires that – what? What did those wires do? Whose eavesdropping did they enable?

The bitter irony of the wires being hidden from view by a blinded saint was not lost on Lady Pamela. And what of those who now could not – and so would not – hear? Would their deafness intensify? Lady Pamela feared not – if they could remember what it was they had already heard, if they had made a note of it, if there were records (indeed, recordings) somewhere of all those mumbled confessions. Lady Pamela wished she had kept notes of her own confessions. The thought had never before occurred to her and, in any case, where would she have kept them that was secure from prying eyes and twitching noses? Surely the whole point of confession was to have done with whatever sins, misdemeanours or peccadillos one had shared with the vague shadow behind the grille that was always Fr Coughlin. At the price of a penance one could forget about whatever it was one had done and have no worries for the future. But did Fr Coughlin forget? More importantly, were there now records, in one form or another, of those largely one-sided, murmured conversations? And were those records not in Fr Coughlin's memory but on a machine of some kind – and whose machine? Was this, perhaps, an explanation of the letter?

The envelope, alone in that morning's post, had exuded quality but bore no clue as to the sender's identity. Addressed, punctiliously, to The Right Hon'ble the Countess of Mountcashell, it bore an Irish stamp and a Sligeach[1] postmark. Inside, on the the single sheet of heavy, antique, laid paper, the embossed letterhead was that of Bicker and Bull, Solicitors – long-established, though Mr W. H. Bicker and Mr St-Hubert Bull were themselves long-departed. It was a successor who wrote to suggest, with the greatest respect, that the Countess might care to make an appointment with the subscribed to discuss a matter of some not inconsiderable delicacy in the privacy of the firm's Sligo chambers which, he informed her, were located directly opposite the Courthouse. (That a town of fewer than 20,000 inhabitants should have more than fifty solicitors is revealing, but presently irrelevant).

Lady Pamela had left Bewdley's rather hurriedly, forgoing the apple pie topped with amandine-and-almond crumble that was her usual treat – as well as being a convenient topic of confession. Mrs Warde-Bax had looked somewhat affronted at her ladyship's feeble and impromptu excuse. But the Countess of Mountcashell needed to think and where better than a dark side-chapel in St Barbara's, though well away from the west transept? In all the years she had been coming here, ever since she had been a girl, her confessions had been regular and her wickedness no more than marginally, boringly, predictably venial. She had, though, been advised to renounce her voluntary affectation of a hair shirt (actually a tweed camisole) since, being designer-made, it was accounted a vanity. Was it simply the boring predictability of her marginal lapses that had tempted her once, just once, to do what was undoubtedly neither marginal nor venial? If ever there were a mortal sin, that had been it – somehow made worse in her own eyes by the fact that she had not even liked Mr Johnson …. had she? Her penance had been costly. Fortunately the Earl of Mountcashell's interests did not include his wife's bank account; nor had he questioned the devotion that, apparently, led to her fortnight's retreat in that barbaric sanctuary in the Iron Mountains. But then, he himself liked nothing better than being cowed. However, as disjointed and unaccountable sounds rent erratically the echoey darkness of St Barbara's, Lady Pamela feared that fate was now taking pot-shots at her and that someone, somewhere, had weapons that could be used against her – somewhere being, apparently, Sligo. Well, thought Lady Pamela, let them show themselves.

Meanwhile she would ignore the letter; after all it could be a hoax. For the time being she would do nothing; but it was precisely by her doing nothing that the trap would be sprung. Separately, from their dark, respective vantage points, Sister Veronica, Fr Coughlin and Mr Scrope watched Lady Pamela's descent on to the street, where the Earl too was watching, from the black anonymity of a suitably superannuated cab.

*... the black anonymity...*

# II

# PAINTING

You may, if you are old enough, recall those baggage trolleys that, in my younger days, were to be found standing casually in groups of two or three on railway station platforms. They were always ready for something but, meanwhile, they delighted in tripping the unwary or constituting an unwonted chicane and a danger to shins for those rushing headlong, their eyes fixed on the large suspended sign that read "Gentlemen". Sometimes they overflowed with piles of slumped and distended mail bags. Occasionally one might be found nursing large, woven hampers of intricate construction, baffling arrangements of wicker flaps, metal hinges and leather straps; cane-work both coarse and fine; and tiny, meticulously finished apertures through which bright-eyed, feathery heads peaked – racing pigeons off on a new adventure, once a suitable onward train could be found. Nowhere other than on railway platforms could one find these low, cumbersome bogies with their shrieking steel wheels; shoulder-high oak T-handles to steer and to brake; and the peculiar tribe of small, gnarled and grizzled men whose charges they were, whose heavy Melton trousers were hoisted almost to their oxters and their waistcoats (with backs of blue and white ticking) tricked out with brass buttons.

That particular day, its being early December and pigeon racing therefore in abeyance, I had the trolley to myself. I, though, was not in transit. I was not waiting to be trundled unceremoniously into the guard's van of a train bound for any of those romantic places whose colourful advertisements brightened dingy platforms and damp waiting rooms. I was not destined to goggle at Glen Ogle nor gallivant to Galloway, no matter how enticingly depicted, by artists of whom I had never heard and

whom, I suspected, would not be esteemed in the art college. ('So, commercial!' 'So illustrative!' 'It's not what you would call "Fine Art" is it?') It seemed unfair to dismiss a painting just because its reproduction was emblazoned with a slogan like "Scotland for Holidays", "Fresh Air for Health" or, less catchily, "Unsurpassed for Scenic Grandeur". I doubted whether the artists had any control over how the railway company actually used the images they had commissioned. As a first-year student I would have been more than happy to produce paintings like those in the railway posters. And I had the means, ostensibly.

Beside me, on the rough planks of the baggage trolley, was my meagre equipment: one half-imperial drawing board; a similarly-sized portfolio (nothing fancy, just two large sheets of heavy-duty card joined with a carpet-tape hinge and secured with three black ribbons); some spring clips; some old saucers and jars; assorted brushes and sticks of both charcoal and conté – and my paint: four pots of poster colour: magenta, yellow, cyan and white. That's all we were allowed. With these we were expected to mix any other colour we might want; in theory we could even make black, but in fact it was never more than a dark muddy brown. Only by rubbing in powdered charcoal could we approach black. Forcing us to use such primitive measures meant we would learn a lot about colour-mixing, even if the results tended to lack sparkle. That was the theory. That was the trouble with students'-quality poster paint: it was cheap and, being cheap, the pigments were coarsely ground and combined with lots of filler. Those artists whose work adorned the station walls could obviously afford far better materials. Their colours, even those whose medium was apparently still poster paint, were clear, bright and fresh. Or did they use gouache?

I was absorbed by the problem of achieving the exact shade of maroon for the railway carriage occupying a small but significant part of my picture. Equal amounts of magenta and yellow with a pinch of grated charcoal looked promising but I was waiting for a test area to dry; that's another problem with poster paint – it looks darker wet than it does dry. I was getting increasingly uncomfortable. The wind was howling down the platform, occasional gouts of rain were driving to within a few feet of mine and my donkey jacket and college scarf were proving inadequate. The raised rim of the trolley's platform, which I'd padded with the army-surplus, webbing backpack used for carrying my equipment, was making itself felt. I shifted, lifting the small scrap of cartridge that was my test sheet, to see it better and became aware of a pair of feet; in fact, two pairs of feet; feet which belonged to no-one wanting to retrieve their luggage trolley; feet that had arrived beside me noiselessly; feet shod in those crêpe-soled shoes known as brothel-creepers. They were big shoes, heavy shoes, black shoes, shoes that gave way to expanses of fluorescent sock, pink in one case and lime green in the other, before disappearing up the spouts of two pairs of drainpipe trousers.

I stopped what I was doing and allowed my gaze to ascend, cautiously, first to the hems of two drape jackets with shawl collars and black velvet trimmings, which, despite the

*Feet that had arrived beside me noiselessly.*

weather, were open to reveal brocade waistcoats, ruffle-fronted shirts and bootlace ties. As to the bicycle chains, they were all too obvious, swinging languidly at head height – my head height. Less obvious, yet glinting in the poor light, were the curved steel tangs signifying otherwise concealed straight razors. Ash was flicked on to my drawing board; one of them hawked and a gobbet of spit hit the barrow beside me. Their faces, when I could bring myself to look, were mean, pinched and ferret-like. Hair, heavily greased, had been wrestled into writhing pompadours, one surging upwards like some arrested, fibrous breaker; the other flopping forwards as if a dead animal were attempting to slide down on to the owner's nose. Both had thick side-burns, accentuating their strained appearance, and drooping cigarettes burned in the corners of their coldly smiling mouths.

I had thought this would be a good place to work. Every week two whole days were spent drawing and painting out-of-doors, irrespective of weather. We were being trained to look; we were being trained to see. Observation was everything. We filled sketchbooks by the score; our folios bulged with half-imperial sheets (paper of all kinds) on which we came to terms with the city and, in the process, recorded its ever-changing appearance as the last of the bomb-sites were cleared; slum housing was razed; new roads for the new motor-car age were gouged through the city's Victorian fabric; the ruined shells of the old fruit, vegetable, fish and meat markets demolished; the trams and the trolley buses retreated into their depots never to re-emerge; and whole railway stations were brutally transformed. The air smelled and tasted of decay; no matter where the wind blew, grit got into eyes and under tongues. We learned to find protection from the elements, simultaneously finding suitable subjects. We worked in doorways, in shopping arcades (those that the Luftwaffe had missed), under canal bridges and on railway stations, preferably those not requiring purchase of platform tickets. On good days, the civic squares and church-yards that might otherwise have been attractive, were debarred by the sudden influx of sun-seeking office-workers and weary shoppers. And, in any case, roosting starlings were a persistent and a smelly hazard – as was the old woman who invariably appeared, demanding intemperately to know why I wasn't 'at the front, fighting with our boys'. She, though, would have been greatly preferable to the two Teds who seemed intent on seeing that I did no more painting that day or, possibly, for some little time to come. I really ought to have found the price of a platform ticket at the other station or, at least, chosen a better-frequented part of this one. Stuck here, at the very end of platform 10, as far as it was possible to get from the passengers' footbridge (itself half-hidden by wet smoke) and on a day when trains themselves had become rarities, I felt more vulnerable than I'd ever felt before. Platform 8, opposite, was crowded enough – at its centre, but not out here at its furthermost end. As for platform 12, behind me, it was obscured by a line of empty coaches that lacked a locomotive.

The swinging of the bicycle chains had developed a new insistence. As yet, neither youth had spoken. It seemed to me that they had no need of words; they could make themselves perfectly clear without. With a flick of his chain one of them overturned my water jar; it spilled across the unfinished painting, rendering it very much more unfinished.

'Ow dear! That's a shyme, ent'it? Yow gorra rag or summat? Yow shud woip that up. Yow wodn't want ter spile rilewye property wudja? Yow cud be in trouble, mite'.

'Ah! And so could yow if yow don't beat it'. One of the race of baggage trolley gnomes emerged from behind a poster advising 'Harwich for the Continent': a tiny man seemingly made of knotted rope. 'And Oi just seen yer Mom. She says ter tell yer: don't yow ferget to gow ter the chemists and get the yow-know-whats, fer yer sister'.

## III

# DRAWN

Surprise all round, he thought.   They, obviously, had been surprised he'd applied for the job; and he was surprised they had offered it to him.   They had kept returning to his motives: why did he want to give up a well-paid and prestigious position (well, two in particular seemed to think it was prestigious and had kept pressing the point) to come to Scotland from London?   It wasn't as if he'd be coming to the most attractive part of the country, after all, however you cared to define "attractive".   They had quickly conceded that his credentials were ideal; indeed, that they were better than ideal, better than they could have dreamt. So either they couldn't believe their luck or else the job had been more or less promised already to someone's friend or relative and that the interviews were only for form's sake.   It could be that someone was now rather embarrassed; maybe not all of the panel were in on the promise.   The idea amused him.

Afterwards the other candidates offered their congratulations, like losers at an election count.   All but one were men and he accepted their handshakes gravely and with what he hoped was appropriate reserve and self-deprecation.      The woman was last. She was also very tall, very slim – in fact, very everything, with eyes the colour of the sea and hair to her waist the colour of old amber. She had simply touched his wrist with her cool finger tips and said evenly, quietly

'Well done', so that he had immediately felt the need to apologise and to offer her tea at his hotel. That was another surprise: she had accepted and did so as if she had been expecting it.

He was back in London working out his notice. His firm had been pretty surprised too. A senior partner had taken him for lunch, a lunch designed to do more than fill in for a missed breakfast and where the carrots were not only on the plate. That they would consider paying him that much more to stay and to afford him so much more responsibility was both gratifying and insulting. He'd always felt he had merited more, so why did it take the partners so long to cotton on? Now it was too late. The truth was: he was about to burn out and he knew it. He'd had enough of London too: the claustrophobia, the dirt, everyone's desire for diversion. The north would be different. There was a job that promised the intellectual freedom he had missed; fresh air and exercise on his doorstep, wherever that turned out to be; and there was the woman from the interviews.

Although it had been he who had invited her for tea, it was clear which of them had the more experience of afternoon tea in Scottish hotels, particularly when taken in the residents' lounge (her idea) rather than the restaurant. It had been a leisurely affair, each engulfed by a voluptuous armchair to emerge at intervals to wrest a dainty from the intervening low table or, in his case only, to grapple with the sugar tongs. Crossing her legs in a way that would surely have been impossible at a restaurant table, she had smiled when he had apologised again for taking a job that surely ought to have been hers.

'Please, there's no need. I was offered another job here, anyway, yesterday. So I shall be accepting that – as I was already minded to do'. Already there was a comfortable ease between them; later they exchanged telephone numbers and addresses.

Those two months, back in London, were busier than before the interview as he tidied up loose ends of projects near to completion; had meeting after meeting with those who would carry forward his other projects; and dealt with his landlord, their lawyers and the utilities. Summer approached and travel got worse. He was ready to go. Mentally he was already back in Scotland; he'd even taken to reading one of its papers each day, collecting it from a specialist newsagent each morning, much to the perplexity of his colleagues. At the leaving party in his basement flat in Hendon (which was another good reason to leave) they had wrestled drunkenly and unsuccessfully with the notion that anyone could want to be anywhere other than London. All their mental maps of Britain seemed to bear the legend, in the top corners, "Here There Be Dragons". For them, going north meant going, perhaps, to East Anglia but certainly no further.

Kate was increasingly on his mind. When he thought about his move, it was she that he thought about. The new job was becoming secondary, as if it were no longer the reason to go, but merely a means of living, once there. This despite the fact that it still excited him and promised him the intellectual romps, meanderings and hill-climbs he had been missing. But it was as though all of this was now a wonderful, additional prize with Kate as the real reward.

He crossed the border at Carter Bar just after dawn on what promised to be a fine summer's day. He pulled off the road and got out, stretching and glad to feel the slight, fresh breeze on his face and arms; he had driven through the night. Before him Scotland lay, shimmering where the low sun was already grazing; elsewhere wraiths of mist veiled its promise. He felt no urge to look south: ahead was what mattered. The past had already slammed its door and the noise had barely reached him. He was on the doorstep looking out at Kate. After half an hour, refreshed and urgent, he returned to his car and drove on. Each mile consumed was another mile closer to Kate – not that he knew where she was exactly.

They had written several times in the intervening period – he in black on white, she in purple on green. Her script was bold, angular, impassioned and would have been utterly distinctive even without the chosen ink; his was a regular chancery. They both, he noticed, used broad, obliquely slanted nibs. They admitted each other to selected portions of their respective pasts and shared the intention of seeing more of one another once they had taken up their new jobs in the town where both would be strangers – although not to one another, the way things seemed to be developing. Over those two months a comfortable intimacy had crept into their letters – an intimacy that he dared hope would soon go well beyond the Quink.

In the past decade London had been declared "swinging" but, if so, he'd missed it. Carnaby Street was simply a tawdry tourist trap; Abbey Road was where his car was serviced; and Covent Garden was still a fruit and vegetable market reeking of rotting cabbage. The occasional copy of *Oz* and *International Times* that he picked up between home and office suggested that some people were having fun, often bizarrely, but he never encountered them; he'd been too busy with deadlines, contracts and the responsibility of spending other people's money. Come to think about it, he never met anyone except those implicated in the deadlines, the contracts and the other people's money. Had he missed out? He decided not, since he might otherwise never have met Kate. Perhaps with her he could do some catching up.

He heard a 'phone ring somewhere below. He was staring out of his open window, entranced at a field of oil-seed rape beyond the garden fence, transfixed by its colour that seemed to belong to no palette that he recognised. There was a tentative knock at his door which then opened slowly and a girl of about twenty peered in. Her cheeks glowed in a way he had never seen in London and she wore her hair in a long, single, braided pigtail beneath some kind of embroidered band.

'It's for you', she said and pointed back to the stair. In the hallway he picked up the receiver tentatively, prepared for some mistake. He had been in the house no more than an hour or two and so a 'phone call seemed unlikely: his mother, perhaps, inquiring about his journey; or maybe the London friend whose student sister had agreed to his occupying her room during the rest of the vac.

'Welcome to the north', said Kate. 'When can we meet?'

Later, after he had slept a little, he drove into the city and found the bar she had described. He parked his Beetle at the kerb-side and, as he locked it, there came the familiar splutter of another immediately behind him, where it stopped. He turned. Kate was at the wheel of a rare Karman Ghia model, green to match her ink.

The bar was dark and smoke-filled, its wood panelling blackened by age and nicotine. A series of screened recesses, each with its own pair of ancient chairs, a bench and a scruffy table, surveyed the long bar where a pair of workmen were in coarse debate. Kate, unfeezed, took his arm and guided him into one of the alcoves:

'Get me a half of Guinness' she said.

'Why here?' he asked as they sipped their beers.

'Oh, it has quite a reputation, I'm told. When the students are back it is packed and you have to queue to get in. So

I thought we'd take a look while we could'. He liked the "we". It reinforced the sense of convergence.

Over the next week the bar became a constant meeting place, although not the only one. She had got digs in the city and was already in her new job; his was not due to begin for another three weeks during which time he intended finding a place of his own. Little by little they drew the curtains of their respective pasts back further, exclaiming at common experience and discovering mutual interests. Neither seemed to have brought with them much in the way of emotional baggage, yet in their own relationship the initial impetus had given way to caution. Nevertheless, it grew, slowly and the touch on the arm became less accidental, lasted longer, entailed the use of both hands and eventually became an embrace. When a kiss finally ensued it was not so much that as the ferocity of her grasp that surprised him.

He was having no success in finding somewhere to rent. Kate, too, already tired of the limitations of her digs, and with limited time at her disposal, was being equally unsuccessful. For him time was running out: his friend's sister would soon be returning for another term and would want her room back and, although those students still at the farmhouse through the summer had accepted his presence with equanimity and had even involved him in their raspberry scrumping, staying on was never suggested. Eventually one of them, a law student, told him of a tutor who also had a practice in the city – who, in turn, passed him on to a client with property interests who, in turn, offered him a whole house, recently refurbished and not yet on the market, in one of the suburbs. It was far too big for him, of course, and the rent too high, as he told Kate.

'Perhaps we could share it', she said and then asked to see it. The owner, an elderly lady, seemed amused by the idea.

'Well', she said 'the house stands on the corner of two streets with a door in each. As far as I am concerned, one of you would live in the one street and the other one in the other street. If you should happen to meet inside, that is none of my business'. Were her motives purely commercial, he wondered.

They moved in. He took the two main rooms upstairs and Kate the two downstairs; his was the side door and hers the front; everything else was shared. In the unspoilt, all white interior they regarded each other's sharp outline, seeing each other like two drawings awaiting an animator. They had hugged each other, cautiously. Later, two removal vans arrived, simultaneously, one at the front and one at the side. Indoors there was echoing confusion. Outside some neighbours watched with lips pursed.

It was curious, he thought, how in the first couple of weeks in the house their paths seemed hardly to have crossed. Their working hours were different, certainly, but he had imagined that she would have been less like a ghost evidenced only by an increasing assembly of bottles in the bathroom, crumbs on the kitchen work-top and the smell of incense that came from her bedroom. There was also the occasional note, such as "Could you bring back some milk?"  Instead of having become even closer through co-habitation, it was if they had become separated by it and that upset him.  He realised that Kate mattered to him in a different way now: this was more than infatuation.

One Friday evening he met her returning from the bathroom, a deep blue robe belted tightly around her and her hair hanging damply down her back.

'I was about to make a hot drink.  Would you like one?' he asked. It was only when she sniffed that he realised she had been crying.  He made the drinks and took them into her sitting room, but it was empty.  He knocked at her bedroom.

'I'm in here' he heard, so he went in.  She was propped against the head of her bed, towelling her hair, but without conviction.  He put down her drink and made to leave.

'Talk to me', Kate said.  He sat, awkwardly, beside her and took the towel.

'Let me', he said and began to dry her hair as he had once had to do for his kid sister.  'What's the matter?' he asked.

'I was at confession tonight'.

'Is that bad?'

'Not usually, no'.

'But this time it was?'  Kate nodded and sipped her drink.

'Do you want to talk about it?' This time she was quiet for minute or two and then said quietly

'The priest said that what I'm doing, sharing a house with you, could be wrong and that I am great danger'. She put down her drink and her shoulders began to shake once more. He held them until the shaking stopped. She turned and held his hand, the same cool finger tips that had touched him at the very first.

'I don't think I'm doing wrong, do you?' All too aware of his self-interest, he shook his head. She hugged him. 'I think you should go now'.

It was a few weeks later that they went to the exhibition at the local art society. It boasted a typical assembly of nervous watercolours and constipated oils, but there was still enough amongst the dross to make the visit worthwhile. A large, explosive, Indian ink drawing slashed with gouts of bright colour only gradually revealed its subject as a nude. Was this why it had been hung in the darkest corner or would it have outshone everything else if hung elsewhere? They stared at it for a long time, saying nothing, as if each were silently feasting.

Back at the house, over a rare shared lunch, Kate said 'I loved that big drawing – the nude. It was so....passionate. His feelings for his model must have been so strong'.

'Like mine for you' he replied. It was out before before he knew it.

*Perhaps we need to draw each other*

'I know' whispered Kate. 'I feel the same. Perhaps we need to draw each other'.

'I rather think we have'.

*Grim Harlin stood at the edge of the small town*

## IV
# AT GRIM HARLIN

Grim Harlin stood at the edge of the small town. The North Sea nagged the dunes on its east side; the links bumped away to the south. Spreading awkwardly, of indeterminate shape and with numerous roofs that fought without resolution for the ascendancy, the house was indeed both harled and grimly grey: grey slates, grey-painted barge boards, grey-painted frames to the multiplicity of windows and, yes, grim grey harling. If it resembled anything at all it was a golf pavilion, though built on a scale quite unwarranted by the modest, neighbouring course. Its bewildering external complexity would not have been accounted for by the relatively simple planning required of a golfers' clubhouse. Rather, it had been a jeu d'esprit (if such can be grey) of a wealthy industrialist in the 1920s whose architect clung to the belief that every room, whatever its purpose and whatever its size, should have at least two aspects. Hence the intricacy of Grim Harlin's plan and multiplicity of its windows.

That such an odd, sprawling and idiosyncratic building should be occupied by just one person was equally odd. She herself was by no means sprawling, being hardly more than five feet high and built quite delicately. In her time she had been a solo concert pianist of some little reputation as well as being the devoted accompanist of her husband, a Welsh tenor, also of some little reputation.  He, though, had long since been gathered in to the land of his fathers and Anjuska lived on at Grim Harlin – a gift to her from (it was said) an erstwhile admirer.  Here she spent her mornings in the music room that looked east and south, playing the Bechstein, before walking the short distance to the High Street to make whatever light purchases she required or to call upon her man of business.  Once a week, generally Wednesday, she entertained two or three chosen friends to lunch at her particular table in the dining room of the local hotel, having previously determined what she would require to be served.  In the afternoons, after a short rest, she went to the other music room, the one facing south and west, to play the Steinway for a couple hours.  Evenings were spent more quietly.

Once every couple of months, however, she gave a dinner party.  Kitchen staff and a table maid were hired for the evening; and an Episcopal curate named Andrews (a Sunday friend) adopted most convincingly the rôle of butler, displaying the necessary degree of baldness and unction.  He was, it seems, equally au fait with divine and silver service.  It was as well that Anjuska was not a Presbyterian.

So it was that on a cold March evening, with the wind blasting great gouts of snow from seaward, I presented myself at Grim Harlin.  Andrews showed me into a sitting room where some eight or nine other guests were already standing as close as they might to the logs burning on the hearth.  We were a disparate bunch and, as it transpired, largely unknown to one another, clearly assembled in hope of that liveliness that can elude a table that is too familiar. We were to be the instruments of Anjuska's entertainment in an impromptu for twelve knives and forks.

The dining room was long and narrow, its length perhaps two and a half times its width. At one end a deep bay, now heavily curtained, would have admitted light from three sides; there were no other windows. The two longer walls displayed obligatory oil paintings of dead game and grapes while the inner end of the room was entirely hidden by a huge, black, oak, Jacobean court cupboard doing duty as a sideboard. A single table extended nearly the entire length of the room, Anjuska seated at its head, tiny and animated against the dark, brooding hulk of the seventeenth-century credenza. The company had by this time labelled themselves and each other: an estate factor recently arrived in the area with his wife; two doctors long married and approaching retirement; a research chemist and his wife who ran a preschool play group; David, a retired colonial government advisor and his wife, the Hon. Calixta (or Alix to her friends); a visiting American academic with ties to the episcopal church and her husband who said he was in "logistic provision"; a lawyer; and an artist. Conversation at the table was animated enough while remaining decorous. Anjuska's formulaic and innocuous opening gambit had been all that was needed for a rolling exchange of experiences both mutual and particular, all sustained by an excellent sequence of dishes, glasses that never seemed to empty and a general humour and a willingness to be amused.  It soon became evident that the Honourable Alix enjoyed a strong sense of the absurd; her sly and sometimes surreal interjections diverted any exchange that threatened to become too serious or any disclosure that might prove too personal.  But by largely mutual consent, it seemed, no one had touched on the elephant in the room – that very large oaken elephant – until, that is, Anjuska was called away to the kitchen in response to some culinary crisis.

'My, but isn't that some carpentry?'  Only an American could have been so gauche.  There came sundry embarrassed grunts of assent to this gaffe, grunts meant to signal that their hostess's furniture was not a suitable subject for discussion.  For a moment there was an embarrassed silence but into which Alix then observed conspiratorially

'And do you know,  Anjuska made it all by herself, at evening classes?  Took years, but she stuck at it, even though cabinet-making and chip-carving are not the ideal pastimes for a pianist.  When she started, she could barely even lift a tenon saw, let alone use one.  As for the dyes needed to achieve just the right degree of aged-ness and patination: she totally despaired of ever getting her hands clean again!'

'What?  Never?  You don't say!'  The professor was mightily impressed.  Her eyes shone with admiration for the tiny woman whom she knew only as an interpreter of Chopin and supporter of German lieder.

'Oh, but I most certainly do' confided Alix 'though I know I shouldn't – and I know Anjuska wouldn't thank me for telling you. Better to let it be thought it's been in the family for three hundred years, don't you agree?'

'Quite so' intoned the lawyer, though he too was astonished at the revelation, as were most of us. But I had caught David's wink: it was, I gathered, a typical Alix hoax. At this point Anjuska returned.

'So sorry about that' she breathed 'but sometimes the range can be a little "Agamentative" as I call it – if you are not used to it. Now, where were we?'

Flaunting her mischief the American woman said

'I guess we were talking about hobbies. Do you have any special hobbies, Anjuska?'

'None at all; I prefer to be serious about everything I do' she replied lightly, 'don't you?'

'In school, sure, but outside of school, well I guess you could say I chip away at this and then I chip away at that. I guess I keep needing to carve out new interests for myself, in a manner of speaking; maybe something to furnish my retirement, if you get my drift'. Anjuska smiled in a baffled but understanding way. The American shot a quizzical look at Alix, who was quite untroubled. Others groaned inwardly before all, simultaneously, attempted to launch other topics. But Anjuska's voice rose above the murmurings:

'You make it sound, my dear, as if you yourself have taken up woodwork. Has woodwork become a hobby, one of the activities at which, as you say, you chip away?'

'I? Oh no, mercy me, *I* haven't taken up woodworking'.

'I'm pleased to hear it! It would be so unbecoming, don't you think – even in America?'

Calixta smiled to herself, somewhat maliciously, I thought.

V

# SLIPPING ANCHOR

Behind the baboons stood a shack. Nev had come to regard it as his personal bothy. There he'd bide whenever he reckoned he could swing it. Supervision followed a pattern, one that seldom varied, every week the same, so he knew pretty well when it was safe to skive, when he could vanish into his hermit's hut. Not that there was a hermit, of course, not even of the crab variety. Zoos house all manner of creatures, but not hermits, not these days. In Georgian times a large country estate might boast a couple of bears in the garden, or an orang-utan in the orangery; a tame leopard might be spotted in the library; and, in a specially-contrived grotto in the woods, there could well be an ornamental hermit, a fancy anchorite. But eighteenth-century private menageries were one thing and the municipal zoos of today are quite another. Not that Nev was aware of any of this. He was shy – shy of people and shy of work: an unhelpful combination for a publican – and one also serving a community pay-back order.

"Mine host" he had never been, always hindmost when it came to a round and, by which time, he would be incapable of standing one anyway or, indeed, of standing at all. For all his physical length he was never long in passing out, although his stamina was curiously proportional to the size of the group. His conversation, however, was unaffected by numbers. No matter how many stood at the bar, Nev's input to any discussion was always the same, never more than negligible. Irrespective of topic, his gambit was to nod sagely as if nothing could be truer; that he himself had long thought the same; or else was about to make the identical point. Since all those present were potential sources of a free drink, why antagonise anyone? He had a way of insinuating himself into a circle, with a razor smile, and a roll of his scrawny shoulders, that ensured his inclusion. And if, on rare occasions, he did offer a word or two, nobody took exception, nobody argued the toss since he was largely incomprehensible (the more so as the evening advanced) on account of his accent. For Nev was an incomer; not only that, he was English, with the unmistakable nasal whine of the saa'feast. Oil had brought all manner of leids to Grampian to supplement the local Doric; ears had adjusted heroically; listeners had become very accommodating. But there were limits, and Nev's delivery fell somewhere over the boundary. The attraction, such as it was, of *The Anchor*'s bar lay not in Nev, but in the pool table, the darts board, the juke box, the one-arm bandit and lager that appealed to none but the indiscriminate.

Things were different across The Square, in *The Ship*, an older, smaller establishment, with neither frills nor food, but solid, with real ale and a staggering array of single malts. *The Ship* did not serve lager; it did not host karaoke nights; it boasted no back-room hoping to be mistaken for a restaurant. Cribbage and dominos, however, were available – on request. *The Ship* was preferred port-of-call for Richard Garioch[2], village boat-builder, carpenter, undertaker, honey-farmer, oral historian, collector of Kelvin diesel engines, prodigious reader and, it has to be said, another alcoholic. Richard despised Nev, so much so that, at least once a week, he would call in at *The Anchor*, for a single nip, just to annoy him by being expansively amiable and discoursing at great length, in broadest Doric.

'Aye, aye, Nev. Fit like?' he'd begin, solicitously, before observing perhaps that he 'aye lookit fair forfauchen' or asking did he 'ken the feck o'futrets, frae Finzean tae Fochabers, wiz fykit wi' flechs?'[3]

Never had Nev made any effort to understand the village: to know anything of its past; to discover, for instance, how the harbour – on whose wall *The Anchor* was built – had shaped the village's history, so much of which lay in the graveyard up the steep brae that led, eventually, to the main road; a past, so much of which had never been recovered. Richard counted himself fortunate: he himself, it was, had found his own father's body washed up on the rocks, not two miles down the coast, a month after his boat had been lost. Over the years, though, many a village woman had been left to grieve with not even that much consolation. But Nev was blind to such things. From the sale, say, of a Catford flat or Billericay villa, he'd acquired billets for his entire family, an income and a passport to idleness and cirrhosis.     And if Richard Garioch's liver was similarly threatened, idleness played no part in it.  He was every bit as thin as Nev, but if Nev was wet string Richard was taut wire; Nev's only exercise was pulling pints and, since *The Anchor*'s beer came in kegs, that task needed neither skill nor strength.  But to witness Richard at work on a new 30-foot keel, standing astride an enormous baulk of oak, walking gradually backwards as, with nothing but his instinct, a fine eye and a lethally-sharp adze, he fashioned the backbone of a traditional fishing-boat: well, that was a display of supreme, sinewy, craftsmanship.

Nev, though, had only craftiness – albeit not enough, eventually, to shield him from the licensing board.     Found paralytically incapable, locked in a store room during opening hours (the door had to be broken down) his days as licensee were over, though not his ownership.    It made no difference to his habits, except to prevent his actually going <u>behind</u> the bar.  He'd still rise late, breakfast on a couple of roll-ups and then drive five miles to the bank at Invermorphie with the previous day's takings.     Too bad that a constable with a grudge chose to breathalyse him, finding him way over the limit even before he'd started that day's sousing.    And he had form.    So that was another licence lost and a community pay-back order imposed for what could, so easily, have been a ticket to Craiginches[4].

*The Anchor* itself was unaffected by Nev's restrictions; but now, every Wednesday, Nev had to make a thirty-mile bus trip for his weekly appointment with litter and baboons, sustained only by a hip-flask.  Otherwise he haunted the bar when it was open, ingratiating himself almost wordlessly with unwary customers, or else he sat by the harbour staring vacantly into the water, a hitherto fairly unfamiliar liquid. This became a fixation. Nev, it seemed, was becoming mesmerised by the sea as it slowly rose and then fell through the course of a day. In bad weather he'd shelter beneath an old fishing boat up on the stocks, further shielded by a mountain of creels.

Nev's gradual withdrawal from human commerce of any kind was neither unnoticed nor lamented; out-of-doors, only the gulls kept him company. Them and a grey seal who'd haul herself up the steep slipway while her moult was in progress, to lie only yards from where Nev sat hunched, beside or beneath the hull of the *Good Prospect*. She was an unusually companionable seal. Richard's forays into *The Anchor*'s bar stopped when his target shifted to the quayside. He tried once or twice to fash Nev outside, but it wasn't the same and he gave it up. Any response would have been better than none, but that's all he got. As Richard remarked in *The Ship* one night, it was as if Nev had become some sort of high-visibility recluse, an ornamental hermit.

'An fit's an "ornamental hermit" fan it's at hame?' his pal Sandy Tamson had wanted to know.

'Big hooses aye had ane' said Richard. 'Some aald mannie wiz peyed tae bide in a cave in the gairden, jist wearin' raags or a pellet, as a curiosity like, for romantic effect like, ken?'

*Nev sat hunched, beside
or beneath the hull*

'Aye, well, A cannae say as hoo Nev has ony romantic effect on me' rejoined Sandy 'but he's sure as hell a curiosity noo'. A few days later Richard came into *The Ship* with a book; an old Rizla packet marked a page.

'Read that' he told Sandy. Sandy put on his reading glasses and intoned

' "Nature, in her wonderful irony, driving out the anchorite to feed with the wild animals of the desert and giving to the hermit the beasts of the field as his companions'. "[5]   He checked the book's cover.  'Hell's teeth, Richard:  Oscar Wilde?  I'll nae gang oot i' the boat wi' ye again.  Bit fit's yer pynt?'

'Is tha' nae Nev?  Has he nae become a hermit?  An' dis he nae spend maist o' his day wi' beasts o' the field – or the craturs o' the sea an' air, at ony rate?'

'Aye – an' he's frae *The Anchor*, right enough.  So A guess that maks him an anchorite tae,' laughed Sandy.

Nev was once again staring fixedly into the harbour's depths.  His ban expired that day:  he was back at the wheel of his car, meaning to drive to the bank in Invermorphie.  The gulls circled above him; the seal watched balefully from her favourite haul-out; and Nev started the engine, released the hand brake and slewed into the dock.  The seal had no chance.

Nev's burial was a fortnight later.  A large wooden coffin was loaded on to a bogie and hauled by tractor up the brae to the cemetery, according to village custom; Richard, as local undertaker, had been responsible for all arrangements; Richard it was had built the coffin.

'Ye've made a fine joab o' this ane' puffed Sandy as the coffin was wrassled to the graveside. 'Houaniver, it's gey heavy. A would nae ha' thocht Nev weighed sae muckle. By the by, I meant tae ask – fit happened tae the poor cratur he killt?'

'Jist dinnae ask,' said Richard, tapping the coffin lid. 'Let's jist say as hoo Nev is noo hermetically sealt'.

Richard's etymology was a little weak, but, as he took up his spade, it didnae spyle his final dig at Nev.

## VI

# THE STEEL CURLEW

Five birds stood on top of Granny's tallest kitchen cupboard. They had been there as long as Lara could remember. All had very long legs. Four of the birds were white and were called ibises. They were made of wood and, so *they* said, came from Egypt. But the fifth bird was dark brown and made of rusted steel. She was a curlew and did not come from Egypt – so the ibises largely ignored her. The curlew was very lonely even though the other four birds stood close beside her, for they hardly ever spoke to her and, when they did, it was only to be rude.

'Dirty brown bird' they would mutter. 'It's a disgrace that we, white ibises from Egypt, have to spend our days with a common bird like you'.

How the curlew wanted to escape. How she wished that she could spread her wings and fly from the top of the cupboard and out into the world she could see below her, the world inhabited by Lara. But her wings were of steel and, try as she might, could not be made to flap. So she stood silently on the cupboard and dreamed of what could never be. And, as she dreamed, tears trickled down her long, elegant, curved bill and dropped one by one on to her steel feet which, little by little, became rustier and rustier. And the more they rusted the weaker they became.

It was a Sunday afternoon in November, a cold, dreich day and quite unsuitable for playing outside. Instead, Lara was sitting by the kitchen stove, watching the logs burn and seeing the most wonderful pictures in the flames as they weaved and danced. And as, hypnotised, she gazed into the blaze, there came a most awful crash. Granny, who had been busy washing marmalade jars, jumped – startled by the noise.

'What on earth was that?' she exclaimed.

'I don't know' said Lara, looking round the kitchen, 'but I think it was somewhere in here'.

Together they explored, looking for what might have made the terrible din. Cupboard doors were opened, one by one, but inside everything was just as Granny had left it. In the fridge nothing was amiss, jars and bottles being exactly were they were meant to be.

'Maybe it was a log falling over in the stove' said Granny.

'No' said Lara 'I was watching the logs and nothing fell'.

It was only then that Lara noticed the curlew. It was lying on its side in the shadows at the foot of the big cupboard. She picked her up.

'Look Granny' she said 'this is what made the noise'.

'My word' exclaimed Granny 'how could that have happened? This curlew has been on top of my cupboard for years and years. Nothing like this has ever happened before'. Lara studied the motionless bird. She stroked its long, down-swept bill, wondering how the beautiful bird (for she knew instantly that it was the most beautiful bird she had ever seen and did not mind at all the fact that it was all brown and rusty) had fallen so noisily to earth.

'Why are the curlew's eyes wet, Granny?' she asked.

'Wet? How can they be wet?' Granny took the curlew from Lara and, putting on her spectacles, peered closely at the bird. She then looked at Lara wonderingly. 'So they are: the bird's eyes *are* wet. If I didn't know better, I would have said she had been crying. But how can a steel curlew cry?' Lara, who understood such things much better than her Granny, thought it quite reasonable for a curlew to cry – even a steel curlew – if it were unhappy. Perhaps, she thought, this curlew really was unhappy.

She took the bird back from her Granny and inspected it more closely: the long, elegant bill, the still-glistening eyes, the splendid but flightless steel wings. Lara's eyes travelled down the curlew's long, crooked legs and came, at last, to rest on the curlew's feet – or what remained of them. Even as she stared, the curlew's long steel toes were crumbling as the rust ate into them, the rust caused by a lifetime of tears.

'That's why the curlew fell' said Lara, pointing at the bird's crippled feet. She stroked the bird lovingly, hoping this would somehow make the curlew better. Granny watched. Lara was a caring child, she thought – while also noticing that the bird was now no longer crying.

'I think I know what we should do, Lara. We'll not stand the curlew back on top of the cupboard. Instead we'll sit her in this' – she pointed to a little box on a low shelf – 'so that her feet won't hurt any more; and where you will be able to look after her every time you come to visit me'.

And it was then that the curlew knew she would no longer be unhappy – and not just because there would be no more unkind ibises.

*46*

## VII

# A CASE HISTORY
# — Part 1, La Finestra —

These events took place almost sixty years ago.  I had been ill –
nerves, that kind of thing – and my doctor had advised a month
abroad, doing absolutely nothing.  So it was that I clambered
down from the Direct Orient Express at Milano Centrale to be
met by a man who, at very short notice, had arranged my stay in
a private house.  There I was simply to eat well and improve my
Italian.  In a vaguely Art Déco café that faced the barriers he
handed me a ticket to Carnate-Usmate (on a branch line to
Lecco) and a card on which he'd written an address – one that
intrigued me.  He wished me well.

Two hours later, having tramped through the maize
fields around Carnate, cursing my tweed suit, my ancient Bergen
rucksack and my even older leather suitcase, I had finally reached
Usmate[6].  Its only street, via Roma, was completely deserted; the
sun had vaporised all life, it seemed.  Flaking shutters hid the
windows of the few shops; only the bar was open, its doorway

protected by dangling ribbons of coloured plastic. Inside, I was met with silent stares from the two men at the counter.

'*Per favore, signori*' I faltered. '*Dov'è la Casa Borgia?*' The owner, unsmiling, paused a moment before jerking his thumb to the left.

'*Seguisca le mura*' he spat.

Outside, I turned left and, as instructed, followed the wall – the high, bulging wall that threatened the sandy footpath. Pilasters, topped by vacant pedestals, projected at intervals. Eventually, both wall and footpath ended. Cobbles cut through to a tall, stuccoed gatehouse, set back a little from the street. It rose isolated, unsupported. Two massive oak doors stood open, immovably, and from its high arch hung a large, rusting lantern. Ornate iron gates in a second, inner wall appeared, unwontedly, to prop their own stone pillars. Beyond, a stony track through rank grass curved towards a large, odd-looking building: was this Casa Borgia?

I stood for a minute in the relative cool of the archway: what had I come to? Then, having eased my rucksack, I lifted my case and stepped back into the sun for the cruelly exposed trek towards the Casa. Crunching heavily along the pitted gravel, I failed to hear her – if, indeed, she made any noise. She wrenched the case from my hand and, clad only in a thin white shift that revealed all too clearly her gaunt form, fled toward the house. Too surprised even to call out, it was a moment or two before I ran after her, rucksack butting painfully into my back, tweeds sticking to my legs. She, though, reached the house quite unencumbered by my case, pushed it through an open window and …. followed it. Only then did I realise there was no

*a tall, stuccoed gatehouse*

entrance, neither in the range facing the path nor in the other, equally dilapidated wing at right-angles to it. Architectural convention dictated a portico, a loggia or at least a flight of shallow steps and then a portentously framed, large and impressively panelled door. But there were none of these; at the foot of a pedimented central bay were just two, tall, casement windows, some distance apart.

I reached the house and looked about. Nothing moved; no birds; no traffic framed in the gate-house arch; no beetling, black-clad peasant women. Within the open window, all was dark: I could discern nothing. I sat on the sill, squirmed out of my rucksack and swung it in; my legs and I followed.

It was cool. In that dark space it felt twenty degrees cooler. My eyes gradually adjusted: alternating lozenges of black and white marble on the floor; a faint patch of yellow light high in a far wall, whence a broad, black staircase decomposed into tenebrae; two portentous, black wooden kists. Opposite the stair a gaping, marble fireplace gradually emerged – followed by ancestral faces in the lamp-black confines of their canvases. An indiscernible, internal door opened slowly to frame a woman, back-lit, still lissome and with golden hair.

'*Benvenuto*' she said, 'I was expecting you'. She held out her hand. 'Leave your bag: the maid will take it to your room. Now, I think you would like some tea?' She led me through to a terrace at the far side of the house; it surveyed a garden once formal, now completely overgrown. There, at an ancient stone table under the shade of a huge oak tree, we drank our tea – it could have been Scotland: a young architecture student, an Italian contessa and her daughter Laura, a nun, home for her birthday. Later it was Laura who showed me to my room: I sensed an unease somehow not connected with that small task.

'Don't…' she began to stammer, brushing my hand as she twisted the doorknob and then, shaking her head, clenched her rosary and was gone.  In the room my luggage waited beside a sprawling bed and things began to feel less odd.    I sank gratefully on to the white covers, pondered my bizarre welcome, gazed at the rococo brass bedstead, the tapestries, the inlaid panels of the high, square ceiling, the …. and fell asleep.

I wakened with a start.  A pale-eyed, filmily-clad figure stood looking at me – the same figure as had introduced me to that house, so unceremoniously.

'*Cena*' she whispered, hoarsely.    I asked her name. 'Ermióne' she replied and was abruptly gone.    Somewhere a gong sounded.

My introduction to Lombardy cuisine followed:    *risotto giallo, osso bucco* and *sbrisolòna*.    In a dimly-lighted room with French windows open to the night-time terrace, we sat, the four of us, at an immensely long table, flanked on one side by monumental, black sideboards and, opposite, agéd still-lifes of fruit and fowl:    il Conte del Corona di San Miniato, the Contessa, Laura and myself.    A large Spinone Italiano called Ercole was suffered to lie at our feet.    It being my first night, everyone spoke English.  I asked about the house and about its entrance – or its absence.

'This' said the Contessa 'is Casa Borgia – or what is left of it.  I am a Borgia – but stay calm: *my* guests *always* survive. When my father died he left the main part of the house to my brother, Ludovico; the east wing to my sister Giulia; and this, the west wing, to me. The gatehouse belongs to all three of us. It would have been better if the entire place had been left to me as neither my brother nor my sister wanted any of it. So Ludovico turned the central part into *appartamenti* for farm labourers; Giulia tore down the east wing; and the gatehouse has been left to collapse slowly by itself. The entrance was, naturally, in Ludovico's legacy but when he constructed his ... ghetto ... it was removed. So *we* now have just two little doors at the corners – and the windows'. She smiled sadly. '*Nonostante*, I love this house. It is where I have always lived – and will always live ... despite...' her voice dropped 'all that has happened'. The Count stared at his plate; and Laura crossed herself.

Amalia, who proved to be table-maid, cook and housekeeper, brought us coffee and we moved to the library where, with chairs pulled close together in that vast room lined entirely with mesh-fronted bibliothequès, the Contessa began to recount the awful history of the house of Borgia. She dwelt at length on her most infamous forebears: Rodrigo who, as Pope Alexander VI had seven mistresses and ten children and who was murdered; his son Cesare who was the inspiration for Machiavelli's *The Prince;* and daughter Lucrezia whose name will ever be associated with debauchery and poisoning. At eleven, Amalia brought us our candles; electricity, apparently, was confined to the ground floor. My hosts' ancestors watched with flickering eyes as I made my way up the darkening stair. On the half landing I paused and looked back, unnerved by a noise, but saw only something pale flutter briefly by that versatile, introductory casement.

I'd slept heavily, so it was late when I came down. Amalia brought me *panini, marmellata di albicocche* and a pot of strong coffee to the terrace. Laura joined me, no longer in her nun's habit, but no more relaxed in herself – if anything, more tense. Later, the Count, with Ercole, showed me round. It was all so sad:  a once-fine house reduced to this:  a gatehouse teetering on failure; piles of rubble where once stood the east wing; a cacophony of tinny transistor radios from the farm-labourers' rookery (once the heart of the house); and elegant gardens now caricatured in weeds and briers.  In a roofless outhouse, tumbled on their backs where they had been for a hundred years, lay dozens of statues, variously dismembered.

'These used to stand on the outer walls' gestured the Count 'but were victims of the Risorgimento.  Now they await us'.  He laughed ruefully.  'I have a worthless title; my wife has a worthless estate; soon, we will all be equal – and ride like this'. He swung open the gates of a coach-house to reveal a hearse:  a ponderous, horse-drawn affair, an ornate wooden scaffolding on enormous spoked wheels, with black and gilt Corinthian columns at its four corners and an elaborately-carved canopy suspending black silk curtains festooned with tassels.  'This, also, is part of the Borgia legacy – but now it is used for all local funerals'. Outside, Ercole howled.  I made some sketches of the *carro funebre*, the start of my intended visual diary.

Ercole howled again that night as, candle in hand, I climbed to my room. Looking out on the overgrown courtyard I could see him standing motionless, eerily pale in the moonlight, looking across towards the gate-house where I thought I saw Ermióne, alerted too, perhaps, by Ercole's noise. But even as I glimpsed her, she dissolved into the shadow of the arch and Ercole began furiously to dig.

I had an uncomfortable night and eventually rose feeling I'd not slept at all. Thunder cracked overhead. It was still early – enough time to sketch my room before breakfast. I took up the pad which lay open beside my bed and looked again at the hearse – a very fluid pen-and-wash drawing surrounded by more tightly-drawn details of the hearse's ornamentation. But there, beneath a study of the spring seat, in a spidery, tortured hand, was written *una lettera arriverà* – "a letter will come".

I was both affronted and puzzled: someone else had used my sketchbook: who? Why? When? What letter? Was it for me? I turned to the next page, a blank, and tried unsuccessfully to capture the contrast between the elaborately ornamented bedstead and the brooding bulk of an immense mahogany wardrobe topped by an array of antique military helmets. But I was too distracted.

Relentless rain imprisoned breakfast in the dining room; only Laura was there. As I entered, something she was writing was pushed hurriedly into an unaddressed envelope. She greeted me warily. Was hers, I wondered, the unknown hand? Would I soon see that envelope again?  Tense and evidently disinclined to talk, Laura left the room.

Sudden crashes terrified my second coffee.  I ran out. Laura was standing uncertainly at the foot of the staircase, looking across at that window through which I'd first arrived: it was open, its inner shutters banging erratically against the reveals and its iron bars clashing on the sill.  I secured the brods and closed the casement, as out in the courtyard Ermióne, ill-clad as ever, fled through the pounding deluge towards the gatehouse. Laura, though, seemed not to see her and it wasn't my place to accuse a servant.

'It must have been the storm[7]' I offered.  Laura shook her head, her gaze transfixed by the window.

'Such things happen – in this house' she warned ' – if _I_ am here'.

*In Casa Borgia*

VIII

# A CASE HISTORY
## — Part 2, The Case —

Laura, harrowed Laura, was I reckoned pretty screwed up. Was that why she was in a convent or did the convent come first? I went into the library to ponder. Its shutters were still closed so I didn't see the damage: I fell over it. A tall book-case was lying across the floor, face down. Had this, in fact, been the crash I'd heard? I pulled back the nearest shutter to inspect the damage both to the book-case and to my shins. None seemed in too much need of repair. To re-erect the book-case, though, would be difficult: its doors had remained shut with all the books still inside. It would have to be done in stages. I managed to tip it on to its side, then opened its mesh-screened doors and, taking care to preserve their order, removed the books, all of which had been on the upper shelves. It was then reasonably easy to right the case. A more interesting task followed: inspecting and returning the books. Most were in poor condition (due to damp and vermiculation) and nineteenth century. Two, though, were much older: *Essercitio di Perfettione et di Virtu Riligiose* by Rodriguez in

Pulignano's translation, published in 1619 by Zanetti in Rome; and *Meditatione del Padre Ludovico da Paìte della Compagna di Gièsu* translated from Castilian to Tuscan by Braccini and published in Milan in 1641. Its exquisite white leather binding, tooled in gold, was astounding. I opened it gingerly and there, opposite the engraved frontispiece was a slip of paper bearing a single word *"Prendimi"*. I stared in disbelief. The script was the same as in my sketchbook. What did Laura mean – if indeed it was she – by "take me"? What was it all about? Why choose such a bizarre way to communicate? I really had to confront her, but what should I say? I would consider it in a bath while ridding myself of all the cobwebs, dust and grime from the book-case.

If I'd known the difficulty my request for a bath entailed, I might well have done without. However, the Contessa said it would be ready in about an hour: someone would find me. While I waited I fetched my sketchbook and compared its inscription with that hidden in the *Meditatione del Padre Ludovico*; there could be no doubt about their similarity or the sense of anguish. But why was the book-case overturned? Even though top-heavy, it would need great force to topple it: pulling violently at its doors without turning their catches, perhaps? But by then the message would have been concealed: it didn't make sense. Could Laura be that violent? Just what was her state? She had seemed calm enough when I found her at the foot of the stairs, despite the clashing shutters. Thinking more about Laura I took from the shelves another, beautifully bound book I did not recall seeing earlier – a Book of Hours, written in French and printed in St Brieuc in 1788. There were no surprises hidden inside but as I returned it to the book-case a hoarse voice behind me said

'*È l'ora. Vengami*'. Ermióne had entered the library silently and was beckoning me. I looked at my watch and indeed the hour, for my bath, had come. I duly followed. Ermióne, as ever in her scandalous white shift, moved lightly up the stair, pointed to the bathroom door on the half-landing and then vanished up the next flight.

In the bathroom, however, no preparations had been made. The wooden lid was still on the tub and the numerous ewers still stood in their dusty ranks. What was going on? If Ermióne had been tasked with preparing my bath, she had done nothing. I left the room. Laura was on the landing.

'*È l'ora*' she said 'it is time'.

'Time?'

'Yes, time' she said 'for your bath. Come'. And she led me further up the stair to a previously unsuspected bathroom where a wood fire burned beneath a copper boiler and a dribble of scalding, blue-tinged water was already filling the ancient bath-tub. Towels and new soaps were waiting.

'Did you do this for me?' I asked, hoping to open up the conversation I wanted.

'Me? No, of course not. That is a job for a maid. My mother asked me to find you, that is all, because Amalia said she couldn't'. She went out, shutting the door firmly behind her and

I was left with more questions:  what was Ermióne playing at? She <u>had</u> found me and then taken me to the wrong bathroom. Maybe I'd misheard?  Did she perhaps say, in her hoarse voice, *è Laura* rather than *è l'ora?*  If so, why?  What did she mean?  Then, of course, there were the messages.

I did feel much better for my bath, but nothing had been resolved.

Dinner that night was not until 9.30, late, its being Laura's birthday celebration.    It was a family party, cousins having travelled from Como, Milan, Florence and even Sicily. Conversation was animated, loud and for the most part, being mainly in Italian, hard for me to follow.   So I amused myself studying the faces, trying to decide who came from which side of the family.   Those with long heads, long noses, wide mouths and dark-lashed pale eyes were, I reckoned, the Borgias.   Meanwhile courses came in seemingly endless succession, poor Amalia at times struggling to attend to us all.   I supposed that Ermióne was deemed too harum-scarum to wait at table and was, instead, busy at the sink.

The company got louder and livelier – except for Laura who, gradually, had become almost silent.    Midnight struck, heralding Laura's true birthday.   The Count rose and proposed a toast.    We, too, all stood and lifted our glasses while Laura, remaining seated, stared fixedly at the table – before fainting. Within moments she had been lifted by several of the other women and carried to her room; the Contessa, with a helpless gesture smiled weakly and said

'*Tensione nervosa*'.   Not for the first time, I thought, empathising.  Ercole began to whine.

The party broke up.  I decided that fresh air would clear my head before sleep and went out, beyond the terrace, to stand beneath the oak.   Gazing over the decaying parterre, trying despite the shadows to determine its original pattern, I was surprised to see Ermióne a little way off, resting her arm on a broken urn and looking up at the house.  I followed her gaze and there, in an upstairs window, her troubled, wan face reflecting a momentary glimmer of moonlight, was Laura staring down at Ermióne.   Ercole, who had followed me out, barked and bounded towards the urn but Ermióne had been swallowed in fresh shadows and Ercole likewise.

'He'll come back' said the Count, who had joined me.

Evidently Laura was conscious again – reassuring but frustrating, since I'd not yet talked to her.  I resolved to do it first thing.

Next morning, somewhat late, breakfast was under the oak tree.  Laura was sitting alone at the stone table and I was about to say something conventional about her birthday and how I hoped she was feeling better, when she forestalled me.

'There's a letter for you.  It's in the dining room'.  My pulse quickened:  were things about to become clearer?  I went back inside.  A single envelope lay on a silver tray on one of the credenzas; but it was not the envelope I had seen the day before. It was post-marked "Edinburgh".   Inside, the family lawyers regretted to inform me that my only uncle had died and that it was imperative I returned to Scotland immediately for the reading of his will. Generous funds to make this possible would be available to me at a bank in Milan. I found the Contessa. She could not have been more understanding, insisting I ate some breakfast while Amalia was sent to pack all my things. She herself would then drive me to Milan in her little FIAT convertible, first to the bank and then to Milano Centrale for the first available train. I sat for a while in the dining room, wondering at this turn of events, before returning to the terrace, my thoughts in a jumble.

'My uncle has died' I told Laura. 'I have to go home'.

'I will pray for you both' she answered, crossing herself. But she did not say 'Take me'.

'I wanted to ask you ...' I began but, at that moment, her mother called

'We're ready! Are you ready?' I took Laura's hand briefly, then followed the Contessa to her car. The Count came out to offer condolences and to wish me a safe journey. And from a respectful distance Amalia gave a half wave.

'Perhaps' I said 'I should also say goodbye to Ermióne'. The two looked blank.

'Ermióne? There is no-one here called Ermióne'. The Count looked confused.

'Ermióne knows already' – a hoarse whisper behind me. I turned. Laura was at the FIAT's luggage rack. Smiling radiantly, fleetingly she stroked my suitcase.[8]

# IX
# TIME

It looked well on the posters and the bill-boards. Sign-writers and printers had no need of narrow fonts. It was easy to say; easy to remember and, above all, short – as indeed was he. It was not his real name, however. There are few in the theatre world whose birth names are suited to playbills, programmes and posters. *Noms de scène* ("stage names" if you prefer) are largely unknown to the registrars of births, marriages and deaths, unless they subscribe at their leisure to *The Stage*, check out *Curtain Up* or read the arts pages of certain newspapers. Even so, they can't be absolutely sure that the entire cast of a particular production would be unknown to their mothers by the names by which they are billed. But such was the case with Dr Time.

If Dr Time had a first name, no-one knew it. Was he indeed a doctor? a question often debated, but inconclusively. Some thought they recollected him in medical school; another was convinced their paths had crossed in a clap clinic in Lomé; someone else maintained they had met the man who had himself supervised Time's PhD at the University of Witwatersrand, meaning Time was not a medical man at all. Less impressionable commentators asked why his title should be any less a presumption than his surname. The truth of the matter was never spelled out; neither was the word: always just D, r.

Where Time was concerned, though, time was clearly of the essence – not in any legal sense, but because of what it was Dr Time did on stage. Here, time was everything or, rather, timing: for it was as a tap-dancer that he'd first made his mark. He'd been remarkably lithe and loose-limbed which, together with a strong, innate sense of rhythm, equipped him well to follow in the footsteps of, say, Jimmy Slyde or "Bojangles" Robinson. Audiences in music halls up and down the country were quick to appreciate his percussive feet and, indeed, his feats – since there was more to Time than his minutely choreographed hoofing: he was no mean pianist; a virtuoso on the phono-fiddle; and a lugubrious raconteur of somewhat risqué anecdotes. But, above all, he was grotesque. It was his natural tendency to grotesquerie that enabled him to combine his various abilities into his stage act. Not only did he look grotesque in his lank, black wig set on a head too large for his weirdly contorted, spare frame; dressed always in his green velvet waistcoat, dinner jacket, bow tie and moth-eaten black tights; his whole comportment was, to say the least, bizarre. As were his stories.

Without warning he would stop his act, whatever it was he had been doing – a triple travelling side step morphing into a sand dance perhaps; or maybe rendering Beethoven's Pathétique on his one-string phono-fiddle; or else something suggestive with a pair of stepladders – and confide to the audience an experience

– such as that, say, originating in a theatrical boarding-house in Chichester:

It was an up-market boarding house – insofar as a boarding house catering for "theatricals" can ever be truly "up-market" given the nature of some (at least) of the clientèle; Dr Time would have been regarded, at that time, as borderline not being (or at least, not yet having become) also a recognised actor; his successes as Père Ubu, Malvolio, Vladimir, Archie Rice and Malone were yet to come. But Mrs Prendergast, proprietrix of The Downs Guesthouse, was ripe material for Dr Time's repertoire; her diction, in particular, amused him. It aspired to the very acme of refinement. Had she, perchance, been brought up in circumstances more elevated than The Downs and wanted that, above all, to be understood; or did she feel that, in the presence of theatricals it behoved her to project; to enunciate with great precision; and to exhibit only the most controlled of diaphragmatic breathing? As for her accent! Somehow she managed to articulate with barely a movement of her lips and as if her teeth or, at least, the teeth she used, were for ever fused together, top and bottom set set firmly in place. The result was, naturally, extremely nasal; even the Windsors might have learned a few useful lessons from Mrs Prendergast had they availed themselves, for a week or so, of her establishment's "Advantageous Half-board Terms". For Dr Time, the defining event had been a column of troops marching past the privet hedge and Mrs Prendergast exclaiming to her daughter (who was collecting the greasy, egg-smeared breakfast plates)

'Oh Goldie, dahling! Do look at the soldiers!' It was the way she pronounced "soldiers". Dr Time appropriated the word and elongated it into a lear. Sōōō-jas! Likewise the accent.

It was Lear – Edward, not the King – by which I mean, or rather do not mean King Edward in a tuberous sense, or indeed in any sense since I refer to Edward Lear:  the artist, illustrator, musician, poet and author of *Non-sense Verses*; but who also had some sensible things to say apropos time, calling it a "leasehold of uncertain date!" and "a taper waning fast!" – as the good Doctor's career was to prove and whose act was variously described as: Pathetic, poignant, tragic, desolate, melancholic, outrageously funny…. and ominous.  But that, particularly, is in the nature of time.

Lear is best remembered for those *Non-sense Verses* each written in the form of a Limerick, a place he never visited although from Limerick it is not, as it happens, a long way to Tipperary (a mere twenty-five miles) about which he (rather than Dr Time) might well have written

> A wee mannie from fair Tipperary
> Was fey and abundantly hairy
> But with long golden tresses
> And penchants for dresses
> Was less leprechaun than …contrary

Dr Time liked that kind of verse.  It could be inserted into his act as, and when, the mood took him.  Depending on how he expressed it, how he wrapped his voice round it, how he contorted his features, it might equally well serve to inject further pathos into his performance or else add a note of levity; but either way it was never, in the circumstances, less than off-beat.

And all the time that he was on stage it was time that regulated everything: the tapping of his shoes, the rhythm of his own accompanying instruments or that of the percussionist down in the orchestra pit, tap-tap-tapping on a snare drum, reinforcing the doctor's time: which, of course, was valuable. Only for the duration of one of Time's monologues did the underlying pulse pause or, at least, soften. I say "monologue" but, really, "anecdote" or even "aside" would more accurately suggest the length of these interruptions, if not their flavour. Here's one, by way of example:

'Has anyone seen my parrot? It's a very large parrot or, strictly speaking, a very large cockatoo. Answers to the name of Paul. I don't know if that is its real name; I don't know if it thinks of itself as a "Paul", but that's what I call it and it replies. Maybe it's just pretty polite; perhaps it's really a Pauline but prefers to keep that private – a transvestite cockatoo, a bird of another feather. Mind you, I've never found an egg in the cage – so I reckon I'm fairly safe in calling him Pretty Paul'.

Dr Time having delivered this from a piano stool would, like a Quasimodo, twist towards the keyboard, strike a C-sharp-minor-seventh chord and begin his own version of the jazz classic *It's Tight Like That*:

[v1]

> 'I got a parakeet, his name is Paul
> Give him a little and he wants it all
> Oh it's tight like that….. it's tight like that
> Don't ya hear me talkin' to ya?
> You know it's tight like that.

[v2]

> 'I got a cockatoo – ' at which point he'd stop abruptly and lear knowingly at the audience to ask

> 'But what interest could you possibly have in my spaniel?'

And then there were his American anecdotes, such as this one.

> 'I once lived in San Francisco: I was a hippie, a Bohemian; I wore flowers in my hair:   belladonna; dogbane; hemlock; wormwood; nightshade.   I wrote protest songs and others took them up, quite successfully – *All You Need Is Gloves* by the Beatles, *Come on, Baby, Bite my Tyres* by The Doors and, of course, Dylan with *Mr Trampoline Man*.  I hung out with the anti-war dissidents, the counter-culture crowd[9]; I tripped with Timothy Leary; I hit the road with Jack Kerouac; and had lunch with William Burroughs (a cold and disorganised affair).

> 'I'd sit on my verandah
> In my rockin' chair,
> Writin' memoranda
> To women never there.

That porch became my study,
That porch was my retreat,
Where I composed my sonnets —
Beautiful, discrete.

'But I ain't Leonard Cohen,
Far less Gertrude Stein,
And as for Allen Ginsberg's beat:
It's less pronounced than mine.

'That Ginsberg was a drop-out:
Long hair & bottle specs,
A patriarchal beard,
Liked unconventional sects
Of tie-dyed kooks and odd-balls
And non-conformist freaks,
Psychedelic mushrooms
And Himalay' mystique.

'But though a so-called beat-nik
Rhythm's not his strength;
He has no sense of metre,
His lines reject strict scansion and even McGonagall's
                              [sense of ….. length'.

Dr Time would then adopt a professorial air and ask

'Or was it an effect of drug-induced dechronicization, in
other words an acid trip, moving outside the normal,
conventional modes of time?' before launching into a mutilated,

painfully funny, broken parody of a tap-dance routine, finally lurching to a clumsy halt and observing

'That, however, ladies and gentlemen, was not an example of dechronicization – that's arthritis'.

The tour was to end in Glasgow. He'd emerged on to Sauchiehall Street from the stage door of The Empire just in time to stop a No 16 tram.

It was his second death that night.

In the Northern Necropolis there's a large slab of blue-grey, polished Bethesda slate. On it, beautifully inscribed, is a single date plus just two words:

Time

Passed

# X

# A SCARY GAMP

It had been a long way to go to stage an exhibition: a little over five hundred miles. In a good car it would have taken getting on for ten hours – even without stops; but in a short-wheelbase Land Rover, towing a trailer, it had taken the best part of two days *and* had included a police warning for exceeding 50mph. In the trailer were my wife's paintings: some thirty or so canvases of various sizes, but mostly too large to fit into the Land Rover itself. Instead, all were swathed in Bubble Wrap™ beneath a tarpaulin. It was crazy. A one-man show is always flattering; but so far from home? So far from the places and people she knew, so far from the places where she already had a market, where she was well-established? Had it been in some prestigious gallery in one of England's larger cities it might have made some sense; but in a small gallery secreted above a library in a Suffolk market town with fewer than five thousand inhabitants – one of whom was my sister? She it was had set the whole thing up. The gallery's owner was a friend; previous exhibitions there had done very well; London critics had been known to attend the openings; its publicity was smart; and the gallery had a very good client list.

But it was ready for something new, something different, a change from its fund of Suffolk watercolours and Essex pastels. A bracing blast of muscular Scottish landscape laced with technically complex etchings would surely act as a tonic.

Whether the gallery's owners were quite as enthusiastic was open to question. But, as the intended exhibition by the local art group had had to be postponed until its members could resolve certain differences which threatened the group's very continuation, there was suddenly a gap in the gallery's calendar that needed filled. My sister Morag (who then knew nothing about art) had volunteered my wife Shona as the gallery's saviour; Shona was flattered by the invitation; so I had the pleasure of towing thirty large canvases five hundred miles south and, I suspected, a further five hundred miles north again a fortnight later.

My misgivings did not appear groundless. A noon opening on a Friday was odd; the rationale – that Friday was market day and therefore busier than other days – did not appear all that relevant and, indeed, by one o'clock barely a handful of people had hauled themselves up the narrow stairway and the girl at the sales desk had not been troubled. Appreciation of the paintings, such as it was, had been largely banal or else a trigger for irrelevant anecdotes; the etchings were passed over with incomprehension. Only the wine bottles got much in the way of attention.

By two o'clock there had been little change and we were staring out of a window at the market-day throng passing by, always passing by. The voice startled us.

'I remember you doing this one'. Shona swung round.

'Marion! What on earth are you doing here?' They hugged.

'My parents live only about fifteen miles away and I'm on the gallery's mailing list. So when I saw your name I thought

I'd come down from town a day early and give you a surprise'. I knew Marion Pine's name – Shona had often mentioned her when talking about her time in Paris as a student in Bill Hayter's Atelier 17 in rue Daguerre. That was there she had learned to etch and to engrave. Marion was pointing at a large abstract consisting of meticulously engraved swirls and parallels printed in three overlapping translucent colours using both the intaglio and the plate's surface. It was a technical tour de force.

'I remember you doing this. We were all rather impressed; even Bill himself was quietly pleased, I reckon. I'm surprised there are any of the edition left to sell'.

'It has never been shown before, that's why'. Some catching-up ensued and I had time to take in the phenomenon that was Marion Pine.

Marion was built on an heroic scale: over six feet tall and with proportions for which the term "generous" was totally inadequate. In Paris she had supplemented her allowance by modelling in various artists' studios where she was regarded not so much as a life model but more as a living landscape. Someone had once described her as "Tuscany made flesh". That her own work should be delicate almost to the point of evanescence was bizarre; surely not the work of someone who had driven her ancient Hotchkiss Jeep round Paris for two years with such brutal abandonment and joie de vivre.

That joie de vivre announced itself from afar – not just in Marion's physicality but in the manner she chose to clothe it.

It takes a lot of confidence to wear purple, plum, violet, fuchsia, carmine, salmon, amber or egg yolk – and all together, from top to toe; even more so if you are a redhead.  She gave Shona a post-card.  On one side a reproduction of one of Marion's own aquatints – a foggy and mysterious evocation of an Essex creek – and on the other, an address.

'My parents would like you to come to lunch tomorrow, if you can.  That's where you'll find us.  Twelve-thirty for one?  Just one thing, though, not a word about Zeke'.  With that she sundered the growing throng that had entered at her heels and was gone.  The gallery was suddenly a darker place but at least interest in the exhibits was picking up.

'Zeke?'

'Marion's lover'.

'And Marion's parents don't know about him?'

'No; nor would they approve if they did.  They are very old-fashioned'.

'Because they're not married?'

'That and the fact that Zeke is from Trinidad, he's black and he's very left-wing.  Marion's father is none of those things: he's the local squire.  Marion loves him and her mother deeply – she's adopted – and will do all she can to avoid hurting them.  So Zeke, who seems very understanding, is kept secret'.

'Did you ever meet him?'

'Just the once. I stayed with them in their flat in the Cromwell Road, after Paris, when I was heading back to Scotland. They're still there'.

My sister, for whom Saturday lunch represented nothing more taxing than a trip to one or other of the little pubs that decorated that part of Suffolk, was in no way discomposed by our decamping: she looked forward to hearing about lunch at Bearly Manor. For that was the address Marion had written on her card, to which she had added "immediately west of the church".

Not until we drove into Bearly did it click. Something had been unsuccessfully nagging my memory until there, on the verge, was the bald announcement: "Bearly". No "Welcome to Bearly"; or "Bearly welcomes careful drivers"; just "Bearly" in bold, black, sans serif capitals on a white-painted metal rectangle supported by a metal pole that stood slightly askew on the grass verge. Then it came back to me, the book borrowed from my local library almost fifteen years earlier: entitled "Bearly – credible?" it was written by one Barry Gryce and had purported to be a true record of a hundred years of ghostly manifestations in Bearly, principally in its rectory but also in its church – the very church beside which we were now parked. If Gryce was to be believed, Bearly had been a regular hotbed of apparitions, poltergeists, ectoplasm and spontaneous graffiti over a long period and experienced by numerous people, but most of all by the occupants of the rectory – none of whom stayed long. When the rectory burnt to the ground in 1939, poltergeists got the

*Beyond the hedge, the ruins*

blame; but the phenomena had not ceased, or so it was alleged. I hadn't believed a word of it. It was all a long-running fraud built on hoaxes, credulity and hysteria, by my reckoning. Gryce himself, a self-proclaimed paranormal investigator, was a fraud.

Lunch had been not unpleasant. The rambling, half-timbered manor house had been an apt setting for a traditional, rambling Saturday lunch. Marion's parents gazed fondly, if somewhat bemusedly, on their cuckoo, twittering and harrumphing as seemed to them appropriate, given their presbycusis. We were now standing in the glebe, across from the house, admiring Marion's horse (she was its owner, not its rider, and entered it at lesser race meetings, not without success). The lower end of the field was cropped short; the upper end, this side of the hedge, was quite rank. Beyond the hedge, the ruins of the rectory still reared above an impenetrably overgrown garden. We'd not talked about the rectory.

'Looks to me as if this field needs more than the one horse' I said, indicating its un-grazed upper half.

'Hah!' exclaimed Marion 'It wouldn't matter how many horses you put in here, it would make no difference. They just don't seem to like it up at that end'.

'Could be they're spooked' said Shona who knew a thing or two about horses, having once ridden a garron across Scotland, coast to coast, 'those ruins being just over the hedge'. Marion was dismissive. She clearly had no truck with Bearly's alleged para-normality. The unending stream of credulous visitors at all times of day and night infuriated her:

'The only ghost they'll find round here is me in my nightie shouting at them to bugger off'. It was a tempting thought.

We'd left the horse to its lonely buffet and crossed back to the church, a small building with just a nave, chancel and south porch, all somehow miniaturised, and with a petite but sturdy tower at its west end, at its foot a vestry open to the nave. Its style was superficially Perpendicular but something much earlier and simpler lay beneath; while lying beneath an enormous limestone table tomb in one corner of the nave, as they had for almost five hundred years, were the remains of Sir Edward Earlswoode and his wife. The names of other Earlswoodes were carved into the numerous stone tablets set in the white plaster walls. Apart from a hooded piscina and a locked aumbry in the south wall of the chancel, the interior was pretty plain and without much interest – although it struck me that it would convert very nicely into a printmaking studio. I said as much to Shona, who agreed, but Marion looked askance. She and Shona went outside once more while I continued to peer at the memorials, the diminutive pipe organ in the nave's south-east corner, the stained glass, the poupée heads and the brasses. How odd, I thought, the distinct drop in temperature as one moved from nave to chancel; it wasn't as if there was any physical separation, no rood screen. The sun, though, I noticed, had suddenly been blotted out by dark clouds. Col. Pine had predicted rain, recommending umbrellas; mine was hooked over the back pew. Lightning flashed above the churchyard's topiary yews, now frenzied by the sudden gale, and cracks of thunder reverberated down the inside of the tower. St Dymphna's solitary bell quivered in sympathy and its blue-and-white-braided rope convulsed against the vestry wall. The first gust had

*My umbrella wrenched from my arm*

slammed shut the south door, the heavy, black wrought-iron latch crashing into its keep, the detonation reverberating in the echoey nave. Above the noise of the storm I could just make out the voices of Shona and Marion, evidently sheltering in the porch as best they could, the porch being open at its outer end. I went to let them in. Seizing the huge ring handle I twisted it clockwise to raise the latch, but to no avail. I tried again with both hands but still the latch remained resolutely jammed solid in its keep, such was the force with which it had fallen, such was the pressure of the gale. Hammering from those outside signalled fruitless attempts to get in. I tried to lever up the latch without using the ring handle but succeeded only in drawing blood. I cast about for something to help me, something to act as a jemmy, maybe to prise up the latch itself or to crank the heavy, barley-sugar-twist iron ring. The umbrella, hanging from the back of the rear-most pew, was antique and entirely manual in operation; it needed two hands to open it, to close it and to furl its canopy around the simple ash shaft. A black silk band and toggle then held the spokes and the furled canopy in place. It had been my grandfather's. Common sense and sentiment ruled it out as a means of freeing the jammed latch. Nevertheless, I plucked it from the back of the pew, hung it over my forearm and went back to wrestle once more with ancient and uncooperative ironmongery. Nothing had changed. More ineffectual hammering on the outside betrayed Marion's frustration and Shona's annoyance. Attempts at explanation were baffled by the cannonades of wind and the sheer thickness of the door. The temperature had dropped again, suddenly, yet I felt no draught. Something, though, was setting up a sympathetic vibration in the little chamber organ: from its corner now came a low, unremitting groan. The red-glowing sanctuary lamp, that hung above the aumbry, guttered and went out.    The bell-rope contorted wildly, lassoed a lone cassock and cracked loud again against the vestry wall.

A momentary break in the storm admitted a shaft of sunlight slanting through the sculpted yews and lighting the window to the east of the door, a window of incoherent fragments of mediæval glass no doubt assembled from earlier, lost windows.  For barely a second I could make out a faint text in an otherwise clear section.    It said "I will laugh at your calamity; I will mock when your fear cometh – Proverbs 1:26" and then the sun was shrouded once more and the text vanished. I wrestled madly at the twisted iron ring and simultaneously felt my umbrella wrenched from my arm to fall to the floor with its canopy stiffly outspread.  And even as I stared in disbelief it re-furled itself and stood to attention against a bench end, its ferrule planted in the brass tray beneath, its ribs all neatly gathered and its silk band tightly secured. And, as suddenly as it had started, the storm ceased; and the two women burst in – quite unimpeded.

# XI

# TRUST

His voice echoed.

‘ "Tomorrow, we shall hear the last of it – for ever, I trust"[10]’.  He surveyed the upturned faces. He gave them a few moments to take in what it was he had just said, for them to start puzzling over what it was he could possibly mean.

He continued.  'Those are not my words, they are not the words of some Old Testament prophet, not even an obscure one, but the words of a fictional character – yet a character with whom, I suspect, we nearly all feel some familiarity, someone we nearly all think we know, even to have met, though that is plainly impossible.  Let me quote my source again – for although he himself was said to have written very little, whole volumes (literally) were written about him:  hundreds of thousands of words which, together, give us a comprehensive portrait of the man, his affairs and his observations over a period, if not of his entire life, certainly across some twenty-three years.  He is, for instance, recorded as having remarked of a but-recent acquaintance "Mr Joseph Harrison is a gentleman to whose mercy I should be extremely unwilling to trust" [11] '. Do you notice anything in common about those two, short quotations, those two comments so faithfully recorded?'

He paused again and took a sip from from his glass. His question had been rhetorical; he did not expect an answer – indeed answers in such circumstances would have been out of order, were they to be voiced aloud. He had no objection, though, to their thinking of answers, to their turning over in their heads a question which, he suspected, many would find unpalatable – not so much the question itself, perhaps, but the fact of its having been asked at all. They, mostly, looked for the comfort of answers provided, not answers demanded – and certainly not conundrums.

He nevertheless resumed. 'What, do you suppose, might "it" have been of which "the last" was expected to be heard the following day?' More rhetoric, not in the sense of its being orotund or magniloquent, but in its requiring no answer since his listeners might now reasonably expect the answer to follow anyway; which it did, up to a point.

He went on. 'The "it" in question was an event or, more precisely, a whole concatenation of events centred about Black Peter: Black Peter, a name that might equally well denote a man or a place. After all, "Peter" derives from the ancient Greek word πέτρα [petra] meaning rock or stone and there are many places called Black Rock. Here in Scotland, Carn Dhu and Creag Dhubh (both meaning "black rock") are not uncommon place names and their equivalents are to be found in Ireland,

Wales and Cornwall. We will return to the precise nature and identity of Black Peter in a moment, but not before considering Mr Joseph Harrison whom I mentioned a moment ago. There can be little doubt, you might well assume, that, in this case, we are not concerned with limestone-calc or basalt or any other geological characteristic that might give rise to a toponym, carbonic or otherwise. Or are we? Any climbers among you will surely know about Harrison's Rocks in Sussex, a mecca for cliff-starved rock-climbers in the south-east of England and indeed named for the eighteenth-century farmer from whose land those eponymous rocks rise majestically – for all of thirty feet, at most. He, though, was one William Harrison. As for Joseph Harrison: he too was in fact a man – although a man to whose mercy one should indeed be "extremely unwilling to trust".

'And yet… what would you make of Joseph Harrison from his actual description?' Since this had not been mentioned they found it impossible to tell. They waited. 'Here, consolidated somewhat, are the essentials: "a rather stout man….his age … nearer forty than thirty, but his cheeks … so ruddy and his eyes so merry that he still conveyed the impression of a plump and mischievous boy." Surely, you might think, there has been a mistake. That doesn't sound like a man that one should be "extremely unwilling to trust". If anything, quite the opposite. The picture thus painted is a most agreeable one. Were such a man to have been found sitting opposite you in even a third-class compartment (for in those days there were such things) while travelling, say, from Edinburgh to Aberdeen, you might well suppose him to be a congenial companion, one in whom you might repose all manner of meaningless confidences. Beware, however. "Never trust to general impressions[12]".

'That too is a quotation from my previous source; and, as I'm sure you will have noticed by now, what all three have in common is the word "trust". Trust was evidently a matter of great concern to the writer in question or, rather, to the subject of his writings, the person about whom he invariably wrote. Even in his shorter pieces, of which there are some fifty-six, the word "trust" appears on no fewer than one-hundred-and-thirty-five occasions as a noun, a verb or in closely-derived or -modified forms. There are also four, far longer works in which there are another forty-two instances of this word: "trust", a concept that crops up again and again in his writing: there being not one, not two, but, in all, one-hundred-and-seventy-seven references to "trust", one way or another.

'I said I would enlarge somewhat on Black Peter. I have, I fear, been guilty of teasing you. Some of you, I dare say, will be waiting to be confirmed in your suspicion that, by Black Peter, I must surely be referring to Zwarte Piet, the very politically-incorrect, black-faced, December assistant of Sintaklaas in Flanders; or maybe some imagine that I am, somehow, alluding to the Black Rock Gorge over by Evanton, inspiration for James Robertson's fine and not inapt novel *The Testament of Gideon Mack*.[13] Or, perhaps, might I reveal that, as your train pulled out of Dundee, you and Mr Harrison were joined in your compartment by a huge, swarthy, uncouth, black-bearded, seafaring man whose only item of luggage was a harpoon? On the other hand, no such scenarios may have occurred to you; for all I know, you are entertaining quite other possibilities. Whichever it may be, you will now be trusting me to make everything clear, to tie together the several loose ends and to disabuse you of the red herrings with which this otherwise black tale may be starting to smell'.

*It is with indescribable sadness*

They were indeed looking up *at* him, looking up *to* him for explanation of his unusual address, looking for a comforting resolution. He had turned away, extinguished his reading light as if he had nothing more to add and fumbled – to spin back, briefly, violently, his gown sliding from his shoulders, to fling down among them his white collar with its two, long white tabs. In desolation, he cried

'It is with indescribable sadness that I: must today betray *your* trust!'

## XII

# BIDDING MYSELF GOODBYE

I'd driven south, over the border.  I reached the city and parked beside the road, a straight, urban road, of the kind found on the edges of cities, with broad, grassy verges, occasional cherry trees and a slow river running parallel on the far side beyond low railings that could never contain it.

For a city, it was remarkably quiet.  No cars passed and, apart from myself, there were just three others:  a man, a woman and a small girl.  Despite having no resemblance to him at all, I knew the man to be my Uncle Alan; who the others were I'd no idea.  They sauntered up behind me, on the grass, Alan carrying a cricket ball and possibly a bat, though I could not be sure.  Then the ball is bouncing awkwardly, sideways towards the road and I am surprised, for I know Alan to be a good cricketer and unlikely to drop, throw or, least of all, bowl it in that way.  The child runs after it but neither Alan nor the woman appears concerned.  I shout "stop" as one would to a dog and she does, with one foot already in the gutter, and looks round.  I retrieve the ball from the road and, returning it to Alan, ask if he is going to a park to "twirl his arm", a silly phrase I have never used before. His answer is non-committal but that we must first find a supermarket.

I am unused to supermarkets. From the entrance a long, narrow, gloomy passage curves to the right past what appear to be wooden lockers, battered and with flaking paint, that reach from floor to ceiling, some nine feet. All the doors are shut; none has a key. Eventually the passage broadens out into an area, ill-defined, where customers are evidently expected to don white, all-enveloping protective garments of some relatively gauzy material. I recoil at this, though others apparently find this normal. I turn away, leaving Alan and the others, and force a retreat bumping and ricocheting into those still streaming in. The door, though, does not permit people to pass outwards and I must, instead, go through one of what look like disused check-outs – about six in all – all of the same battered appearance as the lockers and all but the furthermost shut. I join a short queue of, perhaps, no more than three. None has shopping. It seems more like somewhere one might pay an account or make a fruitless inquiry. I get the impression that a charge is being levied on those attempting to leave and know I have no money; but whether through carelessness or jostling, the old man in front of me drops his coin which I pick up and slam down on the desk to secure my own release.

Knowing I'd done wrong I ran and ran, gaining height all the time until high on an escarpment still within, but overlooking, the city. All around me was dereliction: house walls now no more than two or three feet tall were all that remained of

*A man and a woman with a push-chair.*

a warren of what appeared to have been a mean, cascading, nineteenth-century slum. The buildings had been tightly interlocked, accessible only by narrow alleys and, being on a steep hillside, numerous flights of steps, all in sandstone, all now worn and made slippery either by wear or a thin smear of gritty dust. As I clambered up through the ruins I noticed others, though few, doing the same. Eventually I came to a broader thoroughfare at right angles to my ascent and on to which I turned. Going right, it quickly reached the shoulder of the ridge, having escaped the jigsaw of the stunted buildings, and began to descend it, flanked only by its own grey kerbstones and vast areas of near-pulverised rubble bulldozed smooth, sloping away to either side.   The demolition of whatever had been there was absolute.

I was overtaken by a man and a woman with a push-chair.   If the push-chair had an occupant I could not say.   Both the man and the woman were far taller than I, similarly dressed in long, blue, serge overcoats.   Both had enormous noses, more like bills. Somehow I'd offended them and attempts were made to jab my ankles with the push-chair.   At first I angrily argued my corner (whatever it was) but then conceded they did indeed have a point – whereupon animosity immediately gave way to a kind of mutual sympathy.   His livelihood, it seemed, was threatened by a ban on, or the disappearance of, large trucks (it wasn't clear which) and he needed to acquire a smaller one.   Meanwhile he had only the push-chair.

We went our separate ways, he striking off diagonally across the waste ground on his left towards a ragged wall of buildings further below.   I turned and retraced my steps, up the hill.

I don't remember leaving the road but soon I was back among the ruined houses and workshops, climbing again the crumbling pends and vennels which were once the regular pathways of those who, formerly, had inhabited this rookery. Now, such was the depredation that progress was only possible at all, in places, on all fours.   Occasional, unknown hands reached out to haul me over this or that obstacle; in other places I found low, wire guard fences stretched between slender steel stanchions let into the sandstone which afforded me purchase.

I was higher now than I'd been previously, in an area where the dereliction was somewhat less: the occasional building still reared more or less intact among the wreckage of its neighbours. The footpaths were now marginally less damaged, seeming to zig-zag, intersecting like so many scissors, across the side of the hill, rather than continue with the direct assault. Even so, one had still to be wary – paths could still end abruptly in the absence of any steps, where there was nothing for it but lower oneself at arms' length on to the next level below if one wished to continue that particular course.

Curiously, there was no vegetation of any kind here: no grass sprouting from exposed wall heads; no patches of rampant nettles to betray earlier demolition; no adventitious sycamores sapling out of cracks in the coarse masonry. Everything was dry, dusty and parched, as if it had never rained and yet the erosion of the more exposed sandstone blocks showed this to be untrue: the rounded, part-blackened faces of some, that had been wrongly laid, showing ridged contours from their exposure to storms and others spalling as the result of frost. But nothing grew.

It was getting dark. Beyond the city a mountain range of dramatic height and profile was turning a pinky-mauve as the setting sun struck it through the atmospheric haze. It was time to get back; I remembered my car somewhere down below. After

*From which arose a…spiral staircase.*

one or two exploratory traverses I found the remnants of an alley heading steeply downhill which somehow seemed more promising than the others and I clambered down into it. A few strangers followed me, but after no more than three twists and turns our progress was blocked by a door. Above it rose a building that did not appear to have suffered the general fate. The door, a substantial, six-panelled affair, once painted black but now shabby and scuffed, hung slightly open as if to suggest that the path continued beyond it, into or under the building. I pushed with my right hand and it opened easily enough to reveal a passageway, perhaps four and a half feet wide, twice as high and maybe six times as long, lit (if that is the word) by a single small window at mid-point and leading to another, similar door. The floor was of timber boards, uncovered and the walls of a soft, violet plaster, stained and dusty above a bleached yet dirty pine dado. Despite the aridity outside, here there was a pervading odour of damp and rot, though none was visible.

We filed along the passage, our footfalls hollow on the boards, spurts of dust enveloping our feet. The second door opened as easily as the first and gave immediately into the corner of a room perhaps no more than ten feet square but of indeterminable height. What light there was filtered down from somewhere high above

The space was crowded with furniture of a basic and artless kind, the wooden chairs, tables, beds of working men all stripped of their trappings and rising interlocked as far as it was possible to see. Whether this was as it had always been – as if it had been necessary to utilise every cubic inch of space in order to accommodate a large family – or a later turn of events was impossible to say, although a black-leaded range seemed to suggest it had always been this way. Never before had I seen a range from which arose a cast iron spiral staircase. Barely two feet in diameter and, so, near-impossible to climb, it ascended unbroken towards the source of the light.

Some of those who had followed me in had edged into the remoter recesses of the room. I heard voices exclaim

'It must be a museum' and

'This will help you with your history project'. For my own part I wanted to get away from that claustrophobic cell. Another man in a long, blue, serge overcoat blocked the door and had to be persuaded before I could open it and make my escape along the passage back into the desolate landscape.

Somehow I scrambled, slid, jumped and fell down the treacherous wynds until at last I found myself running down a broad crescent, pot-holed, cratered and with vicious rocks jutting from the baked clay and gravel. A high, curving façade, like a harled curtain, followed the crescent on the left but without a single light in a single window. To the right, the view was open across the city towards the mountains, now a darkening purple-blue. Two young boys on mountain bikes raced and leapt past me, exultant, until simultaneously they collided with the same outcrop and were thrown to oblivion.

I'd reached a patch of grass (the first I'd seen since morning) and some of us took a short-cut towards a clump of scrubby trees and bushes half hiding a fence of tall, steel hoops – much like those that still confine some country properties, but three times as high. What at first seemed like a false trail proved otherwise when a wicket gate or turnstile was revealed behind an alder and an elder – but beyond it we simply rejoined the throng from which we'd recently diverted, now all together on a rough, hard, mud path between scruffy grass and hedges that fed, after a short flight of steps, on to a concrete salient where a solitary man with longish hair and dressed in a greatcoat (for once, not blue) lounged, smoking a cigarette. I approached him, urgently, but he motioned me back: I'd to go with the others.

## XIII

# REMEMBRANCE

This film is in black and white.  You will have to imagine any colour, should you need it.  At a pinch I suppose a little red might be admitted, the red sometimes described as *stizza* or, in English "crimson"; here, though, I prefer the Italian *stizza* since it can also mean "rage".  But the introduction of splashes of red into black and white films has become something of a cliché, has it not?  *Schindler's List* has a lot to answer for.  If you can manage, therefore, without the cheap melodrama of an additional stizza topping, I think you will find that what I am about to show you is arresting enough; that you will discover plenty of material for remembrance without the help of a figurative paint brush and a tube of stizza.  Even so, the word "splashes" is not inapt.

It was a dark place, a place not easily found, being in the very foundations of a place itself not easily, if ever, discovered. Some might have known its name; some might have possessed some vague intelligence as to its location; even locals (and there were not too many of them) would struggle to give precise directions.  Whole armies had passed within a mile or two, quite unknowingly; or, if in deliberate search had departed in frustration; or else concluded the place to be a myth. Such visitors (as did come and go) did so discretely, by appointment, usually without attendants, guided, if necessary, through forest and *heugh*[14] by a boy who, being both deaf and mute, could be trusted, interrogation being pointless.

In that airless space, the single candle guttered and flared with even the slightest of movements: an arm as it rose, but an inch or two, before moving on; the crab-wise shuffle, each step defined by the murmured plea

'*Haec quotiescumque feceritis, in mei memoriam facietis*'.

To each: the same exhortation; for each, a brief flicker. Only their upturned hands were visible; faces faint in deepest shadow. Then, having received, they departed, each in turn climbing the ladder, to make good their several escapes. Even so, the priest knew them – as his reports made clear. As did the entrails of my distant grandfather as they spewed down on to Lincoln's Inn Fields while he yet lived, just, upon the gallows above.

That's a scene that needs no colouring in. No more does the scene that resulted: at Fotheringhay, just four months later, when my cousin Mary met with decapitation – in three blundering, bloody acts.

This story itself, the story I am relating, also has a third act, though after an interval, an interval of some eighteen years. That was an act precipitated by another single act (one that failed) this consequent act consisting of no fewer than eight scenes, scenes of appalling Jacobean tragedy, not least for those intimately involved – and their involvement was intimate in every possible way and in ways you'd likely find *im*possible to credit; nor do they reflect any credit on those who wrote the script, their dramaturges or the stage management. For it was all about stage management, of course. The state's management of the last stages of the actors' careers; the management of public theatre, of spectacles calculated to fill the public pit and to fill the pits of public stomachs with fear and revulsion, drawn first to St Paul's and then to Westminster by the fascination of deterrence; whence the victims were also drawn – on rough wooden hurdles, heads down, behind a horse, jolting and lurching over the cobbles, the target of all that a baying crowd might throw; to be further drawn, then hung and, finally, quartered. Free schadenfreude for the rabble, but no freedom for the eight men, five of whom were cousins, the same five that are also my cousins.

I sit alone outside a wayside bar. It is a solitary and disreputable place. The road is really no more than a rutted track. It runs straight as an arrow across the naked plain, its starting and finishing invisible either in the heat haze of summer or in the fogs of winter; a *bygate* without *causeys* that in summer throws up clouds of choking *stour* about all who pass and which, in winter, drives irrevocably from one bottomless morass to another, through quaking furrows of claggy, be-slobbering mud. It is, perhaps, a curiosity that everyone who travels this way does so, inevitably, from right to left.

It is autumn. Kaleidoscopes of seasonal colour are wholly absent, for there are no trees, there is no grass and the earth is grey. Cloud cover is without variation. The fact that sunrise and sunset are now less than twelve hours apart confirms that summer is past and that winter approaches; as does the gradual change from *stour* to *clart*, *clart* that has *slauried* the legs of the person who approaches. It is hard to say, immediately, what kind of person this is, other than it moves slowly, resolutely, firmly even, despite the treacherous surface and the figure's own numerous encumbrances. Dressed in shapeless garments, layer upon layer of thin stuff, uniformly grey, the figure is haphazardly saddled with various small and scabrous suitcases suspended from bleached leather straps; and is further padded with as many pouches sewn into the outermost garment, each closed by a frayed loop and a toggle. The tramp – for such I took them to be – had on their head a kind of close-fitting, soft helmet, skull-shaped but with a wide brim sewn in concentric rings and turned down so as to conceal all but the lower part of the face, which when seen close to, proved to be beard-less. Wire-framed pince-nez, their lenses dark, pinched what could be seen of a nose.

The voice was that of a woman, probably. The *trauchler* had veered from her course and approached where I sat at the bar door. She held out a collection can, devoid of any identification, and gestured at the battered *white-airn* tray which completed her pendent luggage. In it were displayed uncountable poppies, blanched in their entirety of any colour they might once have possessed. I selected one and inserted it

*Uncountable poppies, blanched… of any colour*

carefully into her tin. One of her suitcases jolted spontaneously, glowed faintly and emitted a voice, the voice of Dick Gaughan. It was his song *The Yew Tree*, the "you" tree, the tree that's been witness to history, the tree that accompanies death.

Satisfied, she resumed her *lang trail tae the easins o' the sky*, but Gaughan's last lines stayed with me:

"And the words of the song were a thousand years long
And to learn them's a long thousand more."

And the sky grew ever more dark; and the wind freshening from the north, slammed shut the door at my back as I retreated in.

*An' the wirds o' the sang wir a thoosan' years lang*
*An' tae lear them's a lang thoosan' mair.*

If ever! I *mynd* my distant cousins, the would-be incendiaries; I *mynd* my distant grandfather, the would-be liberator; I *mynd* her whom he sought to liberate, my distant cousin, the Queen o' Scots and would-be queen of England *tae*. It's all very well remembering, but we never learn. But this time it will be different. Och aye? Are not the forces arrayed against us just as they ever were? Are not those forces every bit as much within as without? Just as you remember the supplicant conspirators: remember their priest. Just as you remember the Scottish queen: remember her nobles and her *courteours*. Just as you remember my distant grandfather's descent from the gallows: remember his torturers and those in whose service they wielded their axes, their knives, their tongs and their pliers, before he finally died. They too were victims, suborned. Remembrance: sanitised to the glory of war and the maintenance of power. Remembrance, the retrospective icing on a gâteau that was mouldy, fœtid, rank from the very start. A nation reflects proudly on its citizens killed by its political ineptitude, its cupidity, its deceit, its corruption, its belligerence and the determination to hold on to power: the power of whomsoever reigns and whomsoever, in turn, controls their rein.

## XIV

# THE CASE OF A HORNY GOLACH

'Thank-you, Mrs Houston'. She left the tray, closing the door firmly behind her.

'Will you officiate, Fitson?' The doctor gladly manoeuvred the girdle and the scones over the fire, then checked the chafing dish was ready for Welsh Rabbit afterwards. In the domed cake-stand a half-dozen diet-defying fancies huddled coyly. However, the samovar (a relic of Hames's secret past) was not an Edinburgh tea-time convention – as far as anyone knew.

Moncrieff Hames put aside his vìòla da gamba. The view from his top-floor window across Greyfriars Kirkyard was invariably melancholic; and the evening rain did nothing to lighten it. Hames had been mournfully submerged in Dowland's *Lachrimae Tristes*. He relished the viol's plangency and his repertoire was exclusively of that period. Dowland's music and also that of William Lawes was simultaneously his consolation and his cheer. For such a large man to be capable of such delicacy, both of feeling and execution, still astonished Fitson. That an erstwhile second-row forward, dressed in a heavy, grey, three-piece herringbone tweed suit, distinguished by an expansive double-breasted reefer jacket; now perched on the edge of a Victorian, balloon-back chair; should be capable of

Egidia Newsman acknowledges Sidney Paget

*Moncrieff Hames*

such musical insight would have surprised many. Even Fitson, who'd known Hames a good while, never ceased to wonder at his friend's abilities: which were many, varied and applicable to situations of all kinds. Situations, that is to say, apt for intellectual inquiry; for the days of physical exertion were long gone and it was his brain rather than his brawn that Moncrieff Hames preferred to deploy.

A reverberation shook the building: the hydraulic closer on the street door was altogether too fierce. It was, though, a useful warning. Hames glanced at the wall clock, its Cyrillic numerals another nod at Hames's past.

'If it is who I think it is, he is early. Best hide these'. A sweep of his arm encompassed the tea things which Fitson gathered into an adjoining room. He returned to find Hames regarding his pocket stop-watch as the footfall on the common stair grew louder.

'Detective Inspector Treadles approaches, he of distinctive, asymmetric step and unvarying pace. I give him another seventeen seconds,' observed Hames, after which, precisely, there was indeed a knock at the door. 'Let him in Fitson, there's a good chap'.

A pinched, uncertain kind of man was introduced.

'No improvement in the left hip, evidently' said Hames, his heavy eyelids not lifting, 'and I dare say you will have had your tea'.

'Well, since you ask, sir, the answer on both counts is "no" '.

'Such a pity. However, we must get straight to the reason for your visit'. If Treadles had hoped for any comfort following his tram-ride up from Leith he was disappointed. But at least the number 10 brought him almost to the door – so close, in fact, that no convenient café lay between its stop and Hames's lair – only Greyfriars Bobby and a police box. It amused Treadles to imagine the one as kennel for the other. Hames would have had no time for such whimsicality, were he aware of it; even he had limitations. To him Treadles was nothing more than another policeman out of his depth – just like Sarnie Gleggs.

Sarnie Gleggs, itinerant sandwich-seller, had been found floating face-down in Leith docks: an unrepeatable event for her but, of its kind, all too common in Leith. Indeed, in her case, it might have been expected. There was a kind of inevitability about it. She had been in and around the docks for many years, one way or another. Old men could hardly recollect a time when she had not been there even though, by common consent, she was not *from* there. She had, it was believed, "come off a boat" – but where the boat had come from no-one knew and she herself had never said, even supposing she could remember. Her memory had never been good, as the Leith police had frequently discovered, but of late her mental faculties in general appeared largely to have deserted her. If any could recollect her days as licensee of The Black Spigot, in a dismal corner of Lumsden

Vennel, they would be loath to admit it. In any case, her tenure had been short, licensing board and magistrates both having come down heavily upon her, like so many of her clients. Since release, she had eked a precarious existence from a single room in Tolbooth Wynd, retailing day-old sandwiches (acquired from a bakers in Henderson Street) to the unwary. Later, when the bakers refused further credit, she began making her own, which did nothing for her sales. And so, an increasingly dilapidated Sarnie Gleggs, in her fishwife's garb of voluminous striped skirts and numerous ragged shawls, added a certain colour to the Leith quayside as she edged from doorway to doorway with her wicker basket of savage baps strapped to her bosom, trying to dodge the showers and entice the unsuspecting. In that, at least, she was unchanged.

It was hard to say how long it was before anyone missed her or, rather, noticed her missing. Even then, her absence did not immediately conflate with her being *missing – away*, perhaps, but not therefore *missing*. A week passed and eventually someone wondered aloud about Sarnie Gleggs's whereabouts, briefly and too late: her body floated to the surface the following day. That she had been immersed for many days was not in doubt, her ripped skirts presumably trapped by a lost anchor and her wicker basket likewise hooked. Given her increasingly erratic behaviour and irregular lifestyle, an unfortunate accident seemed not unrealistic; but the Procurator Fiscal, unconvinced, asked the police to investigate further. Their initial findings had vindicated him: Sarnie Gleggs had not been alive when she entered the uninviting water. So what was the explanation?

Since, on the face of it, corpses don't throw themselves into the ocean: how did a dead Sarnie Gleggs come to be floating in twenty feet or more of contaminated seawater? This was the problem that DI Treadles was wrestling with. Such questions as: − when did she enter the water? Did she enter the water at the spot where she was found? How long before entering the water had she died? Above all: how exactly did she die? − were all as yet unanswered. On one point only could Treadles be certain: Sarnie Gleggs had not killed herself. So who had − and how? For the autopsy had revealed nothing, apart from the absence of water in her lungs! There were no external injuries nor even the slightest sign of a struggle. Dockers, many of whom had experience of Leith's treatment of human flotsam, jetsam, lagan and derelict, agreed that the corpse would not have shifted far, once immersed. Sarnie Gleggs may well have been approaching dereliction herself but Treadles doubted she met the term's legal definition: of abandonment on account of her condition.

Treadles had shared his puzzlement with Hames. His consultation had been strictly off-the-record, but such collaboration was not unknown and, having often proved illuminating, was tolerated − providing the flow of information was (as far as practicable) one-way. That suited Hames. He preferred to reach his own view rather than be fed someone else's. So he had simply read the autopsy report; viewed the body; and stood silently thinking on the very rim of the dock. Fitson, whose appearance was both less formidable and less well-kent, had been deputed to ask questions of anyone prepared to share whatever recollections they had of Sarnie Gleggs. In this respect the doctor's consulting-room manner, his gentle probing and his seemingly innocent, sympathetic questions were, as ever, key to the release of a torrent of information unwittingly provided. And if those questioned assumed they'd been talking to the press; or to a distant and estranged relative or friend of the deceased; Fitson felt no need to disabuse them, though avoiding actual fabrication.

Something that Bella McCandlish said had not seemed all that important – just one more glimpse of Sarnie Gleggs's ramshackle lifestyle. Bella McCandlish it was who, from the back door of the baker's shop, supplied Sarnie Gleggs latterly with materials for making a meagre living – Bella McCandlish being someone who abhorred waste, particularly if it could be transformed into a few coins for her own pocket. Their furtive, daily transactions would have been wordless had Bella not felt it incumbent always to ask

'And how are you, the day, Sarnie?' the enigmatic reply being, invariably,

'I never felt better'. But for the two or three weeks before her disappearance, Sarnie's response had been to touch the left side of her head and complain of intermittent pain. Tommy Rizzo, a bookie's runner generally found sheltering in a close on Shore Street, saw everything but embraced omertà –

until Dr Fitson convinced him that he was not a policeman and interested only in Sarnie Gleggs, not Tommy Rizzo. Well, yes, he eventually conceded, he knew Sarnie Gleggs by sight, not, he'd hastened to add, that he ever had any dealings with her. In any case, the nature of his work meant he needed to disappear, at times, into the network of back courts behind Shore Street until he got the "all-clear". But he'd seen enough to know that something in her head was troubling her – pain, rather than worry, he thought … maybe both. She was beginning to walk unsteadily and would occasionally collide with quayside bollards or trip for no obvious reason. Fitson knew that, despite her poor living conditions Sarnie Gleggs had been relatively fit, or as fit as a woman of her age might hope. She had not been wasting away.

Hames, to Treadle's perplexity, had looked closely at Sarnie Gleggs's room. Nothing had been touched since she herself had left it and the fœtid air was further tainted by the smell of rotting fruit in a bowl on the tiny table. The fruit interested Hames, as did the grubby bolster-cover on her unmade and none-too-clean bed. He'd taken the cover away for closer investigation and now held it up for Treadles to see, pointing to a small stain.

'Blood' he said, 'Sarnie Gleggs's blood. But not only blood. There was also this which I have examined, minutely'. He produced a small glass phial that at first appeared empty but actually contained a tiny fragment of something brown. 'I initially supposed this to be no more than a flake of dried blood, signalling, perhaps, a ruptured eardrum. However, it turns out to be *exuviæ*…' Treadles looked blank. '… whose source, I think, is the cause, directly or indirectly, of Sarnie Gleggs's death'.

'So, where did it come from? What is it?'

'Did you not wonder about the fruit?'

'No. Should I have done?'

'They say that in Glasgow, if your corner shop sells any kind of fruit you must stay in a very posh area – the kind of area that does not have corner shops. Leith, by contrast, has any number of corner shops so fruit, there, must be a rarity – as Dr Fitson will confirm, having checked untold wee shops thereabouts'. Hames looked quizzically at Fitson who shook his head and mourned

'Not so much as an apple'.

'As it happens, the fruit's source (however intriguing that may be) is not what matters. What does matter is what that bowl of fruit, probably past its best when Sarnie Gleggs acquired it, also contained – something…' (he produced another small phial) '…of which this is an example'.

'Is that also … what did you call it? *Exuviæ*?'

'It's where the *exuviæ* originated'.

'So what is this… *exuviæ* and where's it come from?'

'It's from the late Sarnie Gleggs's otic secretion – yet not from the late Sarnie Gleggs. She merely made it possible by unknowingly harbouring one of these'. He passed the second phial to Treadles who stared at its contents with sick amazement.

'You mean…?'

'Indeed. That first phial contains a fragment of the moulted exoskeleton (the *exuviæ*) of a beastie like this, a beastie favouring both decaying fruit and dark crevices, no doubt still burrowing its way into Sarnie Gleggs's brain. For it was once part of the external casing of an earwig – the case of a horny golach'.

## XV

# CURTAINS

He'd removed his prostheses; Raoul was back in his cage; his working schmatta were again in their vacuum-sealed bag, out on the slates.

He'd gleaned little of use that evening. Even on the right bank, restaurants were mostly empty; food supplies were uncertain; and left bank events could spread without warning. Still, some restaurateurs had paid him well to move on; diners objected to his grotesque pantomime with a large rat, right outside their windows. He had, though, discovered where certain people dined that night – far from the violence towards which he was heading. A *clochard* no longer: now, in his tightly belted raincoat, a passable post-grad student.

He'd locked the door of his bolt-hole, shimmied, half crouching, along the snaking passage and walked down a floor to the fifth, braving the shared w.c. *en route*. Time was short. The handbill said 9pm; it was already 8.15. He wanted to know more about this: it could be something; it could be nothing. The location intrigued him. In such a mean passageway, the given number was likely a back door; but whose? Which grand building had its postern in that tangle of narrow alleys and yards that scratched at the boulevard's back-side? More importantly: who was responsible? Anyone they should know about? Were they already known? Whoever, they produced superior flyers: thick paper, a simple, geometric image overprinted three times with differing transparency; a bold black title and some typeset text. Paris was awash with protest flyers, mostly pretty amateur; this was different. Then there was the title – *Les Voiles*. *"Voile"*, has many meanings: veil, sail, curtain, net curtain, fog, shroud…. and more. Which was this? The image suggested sails but might also represent, say, cloaks. And what of *"Exécution"*? Again, a word of many meanings …. realisation, performance, implementation, fulfilment …. despatch. *Les Paravents*, Jean Genet's play, had sprung to mind. In English its title is *The Screens*. That's what they call net curtains in Aberdeen – he remembered his exchange year. It could be nothing. On the other hand, Genet's supposedly un-performable $7\frac{1}{2}$ hour play needing 27, huge, interchangeable screens had waited twelve years for its first French production, exactly two years earlier at l'Odéon. Was there a connection, or was his imagination running wild? Only one way to find out, and his way from the eleventh to the fourteenth might be tricky, once he'd crossed the river.

On the bridge his nose readily detected the Latin Quarter. Smoke from smouldering fires and the sour smell of burnt-out vehicles hung in the air. Shouts and chants were becoming louder, more insistent, echoing above the narrow streets corseted by Haussmann's boulevards, approaching the Panthéon – streets he'd to navigate to reach passage de la Main-d'Argente. Some people were being sucked towards the noise; others, mostly in pairs, were heading away, casualties and carers, the contused and the confused. At first just piles of uncollected rubbish blocked the road; then abandoned barricades of savaged trees, uprooted signs, tree-root grilles and material "salvaged" from building sites; after that the casual litter of upturned and torched cars, all naked scorched metal and melted plastic. The din of confrontation was still some little way ahead, but knots of students were lustily dislodging *pavés* with picks and crowbars to replenish their arsenals. Steel roller shutters were dropped and padlocked emphatically over the doors and windows of the small bars and cafés. Every accessible wall carried graffiti attacking equally: the USA in Viet Nam; de Gaulle's government in France; and the fossilised attitudes and practices of the *Sorbonne*. Philosophy replaced commonplace crudity:

*Sous les pavés, la plage*     Beneath the cobbles, the beach;

*Il est interdit, d'interdire*     Forbidding is forbidden;

*Soyons réalistes, exigeons l'impossible*

　　　　　　　　Be realistic, demand the impossible.

　　　Armoured buses, the ubiquitous transport of the civilian riot police, the hated C.R.S, lined boulevard Saint-Germain; in Paris the C.R.S. were loathed and feared. No-one could forget their violent, indiscriminate, rampaging slaughter of a hundred

*117*

unarmed Algerians, in Paris itself, only seven years earlier. It had been covered up. News reports had been comprehensively censored. The numerous, badly beaten corpses that surfaced in the Seine were attributed to Algerian factional infighting. De Gaulle had, just now, declared an amnesty in respect of earlier C.R.S. "exploits". Why? Why now? (Mind you, there were questions about his own crowd.) Ahead, something was happening in place Maubert. He didn't need to go that far. He turned off left and threaded his way towards the Sorbonne. Everything was suddenly much louder. Somewhere close, above the crescendo of rhythmic shouting, spat the fractured attack of grenade fire. Emerging on to rue des Écoles he found himself behind a broken phalanx of C.R.S. advancing stutteringly under a hail of stones: the sinister C.R.S. in black helmets with distinctive Mohican stripes, visors down, dark blue uniforms, shiny black capes, batons swinging, reloading their grenade launchers. A water cannon trundled past as he backed into a doorway. Student protection though was limited to the odd motor-cycle helmet; their dress was the same as for lectures. Only a slovenly heap of abandoned bicycles, mopeds, flags and other scavenged detritus stood between them and the advancing C.R.S. – that and the occasional Molotov cocktail propelled with nothing more than main force. Two *ambulancières*, with a furled stretcher, ran past his hiding place towards a burning figure, victim of a petrol bomb. Tear gas eddied back towards the C.R.S.; their shields were no defence. As the noise escalated further, he made a dash for the far side. He'd other things to do; spectating was unsafe.

The blow to his shoulder should have felled him, but his impetus took him on, beyond the grasp of the riot cop who'd

lagged behind in a *pissoir*. His student get-up was evidently too convincing; he'd be given no chance to share his true credentials with the lumbering, armed *perdreau* trying to capture him.

He distanced himself fast from the stramash in rue des Écoles, zig-zagging very nearly to passage de la Main-d'Argente. Here it was strangely quiet.

*Who'd lagged behind in a pissoir*

The clashes barely half a kilometre away were now muffled by intervening buildings. His shoulder throbbed. No squash for a fortnight, that was for sure. It didn't bother him: he didn't play squash. The passage itself was narrow, paveed, with channels on either side. Openings in its high, peeling, stuccoed walls were all either barred or shuttered. He found number 27 in a shallow recess, together with a man dressed entirely in black.

'*Les Voiles?*' he asked. Shown the hand-bill, he opened the door. 'Go right to the top'.

He could see nothing. Slowly his eyes adjusted. A stair, he discovered, rose in short, equal flights between brick walls, turning 90° left at each quarter landing where a single, smoky flare burnt. At the eighth turn hung a heavy, richly embroidered tapestry. Another black-clad figure accosted him, gesturing lavishly:

> *My hangings all of Tyrian tapestry;*
> *In ivory coffers I have stuffed my crowns,*
> *In cypress chests my arras counter ... points.*[15]

He played on the word "counterpoints", then drew aside the heavy curtain to reveal the next flight, somewhat more brightly lighted. Four more brought another curtain, thinner but elaborately tasseled. Scant light escaped that portière's folds as its black-clad sentinel stepped forward, drew it aside and declaimed

> *The fringèd curtains of thine eye advance,*
> *And say what <u>thou</u> seest yond.*[16]

And, indeed, he could now see somewhat better: flares increased in number as he ascended another four turns to where fine lace was hung. Through it, lights flickered and danced. This time the attendant summoned Baudelaire:

> *And when old Winter puts his blank face to the glass,*
> *I shall close all my shutters, pull the curtains tight,*
> *And build me stately palaces by candlelight.*[17]

He reckoned he'd climbed almost to the top of the building, whatever it was. Even so, it took another eight turns of the stair, now shimmering under numerous candelabra, to end his ascent. A black-swathed African, silhouetted against a brilliantly back-lit gauze, greeted him paraphrasing Othello:

> *O come in, [Monsieur] –*
> *Soft … let me the curtains draw…*

which he did to reveal the back row of a steep theatre balcony. He was in "the gods". The house lights were full on. There were perhaps no more than a hundred seats and around half were taken. The auditorium was small and shabby; junk of all kinds cascaded over the rows in the circle below. The stalls, as far as he could see, had been stripped out and were completely bare. The stage, its apron apart, was hidden by the fire safety curtain. He banged down a seat, disturbing ancient dust. The audience was silent, almost apprehensive. It was not quite nine. He'd be the last to be inducted.

The house lights dimmed and Rilke's words were projected on to the "iron":

> *Who has not sat before his own heart's curtain?*
> *It lifts: and the scenery is falling apart.*[18]

With premonitory creaks the iron was slowly cranked out of view, above the proscenium, revealing a stage utterly undressed. There <u>was</u> no scenery – just a vast white back-cloth. From the grid three powerful white crossing spots focussed on a point downstage, centre-right, but not overlapping entirely. Into this radiant pool toddled a Charlie Chaplin figure who parodied, grotesquely, Chaplin's own drollery before holding up a gloved hand and in a voice surely more Chaliapin than Chaplin addressed "the gods" with Chaplin's own words

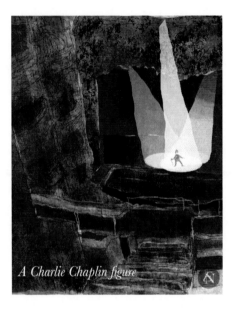

*A Charlie Chaplin figure*

*Life is a play that does not allow rehearsal.*
*So, sing, cry, dance, laugh and live intensely,*
*before the curtain closes*
*and the piece ends with no applause.*

Then, a blitz of blinding light, before, with silent roar, all was crushed by cryptic, starless night.

## XVI

# THE BEAST OF BALNAMOON

That my aunt's mother was a MacPhee should be neither here nor there. But *her* mother was a Robertson, which, by some, would be accounted worse. And as for two great-grandfathers both being Stewarts – well, "tinkler chiels" don't come with a finer heritage than that – if, that is, you yourself are a "summer walker". That's what the crofters of the north-west Highlands called "travelling folk", the itinerant tinsmiths, hawkers, pearl-fishers and horse-dealers who made their living "on the road". They were not gypsies but indigenous, Gaelic-speaking Highlanders. Today, the difference between travelling folk and Romanies is lost on most people. To their eyes there's nothing to choose between them – they're all the same: work-shy; evasive; not to be trusted – particularly if they're Robertsons or MacPhees.

So what credence should I place in the story that follows or, at any rate, certain elements of it;  the story behind the *Press & Journal's*[19] headline "The Beast of Balnamoon"; a story told me by my aunt's mother, Lizzie MacPhee?  Perhaps when I've told *you* the story you can judge for yourselves.

Balnamoon[20] lies at the very northern edge of Strathmore in the county of Angus.  The name has no lunar connotations – it's a corruption of Gaelic and means "homestead in the bog".  That bog was drained centuries ago and the large house now standing there is flanked on three sides by good farmland; but to the north the land rises steeply to a nigh-thousand-foot high ridge distinguished by what remains of two immense Pictish forts called the Caterthuns: the White Caterthun[21] and the Brown Caterthun.

The MacPhee tribe had been camped at Balnamoon since midsummer.  Their bow-tents stood hidden from the house itself by more than a quarter-mile of dense woodland.  The Carnegy-Arbuthnots were glad of the travellers' seasonal labour (war-time having slashed their own forces) but preferred, nevertheless, to see as little of the MacPhees as possible.  So, while Balnamoon's owners came and went by the main drive to the west, the MacPhees and their assorted dogs, horses and children were relegated to the infinitely longer farm track, invisible from the house.  Not that Lizzie's wee sister Maggie was bothered.  When not howking tatties or picking berries with her older siblings, she was free to roam, to explore.  She might not have been able to read like those ferm-toun bairns who taunted her; but could they snare rabbits?  Would they be trusted to lead a horse to the blacksmith?  Small though she was, she had her father's way with horses.  They cared nothing for his hideous disfigurement.  They knew nothing of the explosion.  No-one knew, for certain, who had lobbed the petrol-bomb into the campfire as Angus dozed by its embers, wife and children already asleep in the tent.  As for Maggie, she had no earlier memory of her father with which to compare.

She had led the garron the mile or so from their encampment to the smiddy at Tigerton[22], beside Menmuir.  Even though it was a longer walk, she liked it better than the smiddy at Mill of Balrownie: the Tigerton smith, the local *seanachaidh*, was friendlier; her father took horses there for the more demanding jobs.  Maggie didn't have to be told there would be a long wait – the line of beasts already tied to the fence was explanation enough.

'Come back to Tigerton, the back o'three' the smith had said.  Maggie had looked blank.  'Fan the sun's abuin the bell-heid o' Menmuir kirk' he added, pointing.  She understood that.  What she'd never understood was where the tigers were, the tigers that surely gave the tiny clachan its name.  Tigers, she did know, were big cats – her father had told her that:  so could she go and look for one while she was waiting?  She'd seen Scottish wild cats in the woods over by Pitlochry and they'd seemed quite big, so to see a tiger would be fair byous.  The smith watched her with quiet amusement as she rehearsed her question, finding words for it that he would understand, rather than words she'd use with her tribe. The smith admitted he'd never seen one himself, being more interested in "these beasts", gesturing at the horses, but, pointing now at the steep hillside beyond the smiddy, asked Maggie if she knew what it was called.

'Aye' she answered 'it's cried the Caterthun'.

'An' whit for d'ye think it's cried that?" He'd no need to say more. O coorse! *Cat*erthun! Fit a gaup! She should have jaloused that for herself.

The track past the smiddy door headed north, climbing steadily past Gallows Hillock where, not two centuries before, the lairds of Balnamoon hanged those so condemned in their own barony court. It then veered left to ascend steeply to the shoulder of the ridge before turning sharp right to follow the very ridge itself, with braw views north across the valley of the West Water to the foothills of the Grampians; Gallows Wood dropped away to the right. But Maggie had no eyes for any of this: they were alert only for signs of tiger. Such spoor as she spotted appeared to be principally rabbit, sheep, fox, badger, red deer, stoat and pine marten: nothing unusual; no unknown beasts. By the time she'd made it to the top she was hot and tired; she cooried in the shelter of the vast, tumbled wall that ringed the summit. Through a gap she spied Balnamoon a mile and a half to the south and 750 feet below; through the same gap she'd be well-able to spot any tiger.

She had not expected tigers to talk. Yet the gruff voices of which she slowly became aware were not unintelligible. One was saying that, the battle[23] being lost, they must slaughter their own wives and children and set fire to their own homes; the other that they should simply scatter. That didn't sound like tiger-talk. Maggie struggled to see them, but found herself stuck. Other disembodied voices reached her speaking of 4000 slaughtered[24] on the plain below, including Œngus their king.

A helmeted, bearded man was standing over her, holding a magnificent white beast by its bridle. Gathered at the waist by a leather belt, his knee-length, pleated, wide-sleeved linen tunic was the colour of crocus. Over it he'd a kind of padded cow-hide jerkin daubed in pitch. He rested on an immense sword; on his shield was a picture of another shield showing two big cats, rearing up.

'*Is mise an tìgear*'[25] he said, meaning "I am the tiger". And even though he'd addressed her in her own tongue Maggie found herself unable to speak, unable ask how *he* could be a tiger. And then he was gone – to be replaced by another soldier[26], astride another fine white beast. He too wore a long, pleated, yellow tunic; but also trews and his mantle was of fine, knitted chain. On his shield was a bird the like of which Maggie had never seen: all blue, its enormous wings outstretched, its cruel beak, savage talons and curling tongue all red. He put his fingers to his lips and told her

'You haven't seen me. Tell no one – only that Culloden was lost'. With that, he rode away north pursued by thick mist out of which appeared a black-clad minister astride a donkey. He demanded harshly

'Which way did Balnamoon go?' To which Maggie replied

'*Chan eil mi a'tuigsinn*'.[27] No, she did not understand: after all, how could somewhere go anywhere? The dark cloud now shrouded the Caterthun and Maggie knew she must get back, but something still trapped her legs – nothing would free them: she was still there when a troop of red-coated soldiers marched out of the cloud, going back the way, with the man in trews and chain armour bound helpless to his fine beast and a smirking minister tagging along at the tail. Maggie called out

'*Cha b'e mise*' ('It wasn't me') but no-one heard her. By now the wind had risen and the dark clouds were swept away. Maggie was chilled. She tried again to move – this time with no difficulty. The sun, visible once more, had moved across the sky much further than Maggie would have thought possible. She had to get back. The blacksmith would be wondering where she was. She hurried, running, hopping, skipping, leaping down the ridge, along the edge of the wood whose name she did not know, past the hillock whose name she did not know but which, for some reason, made her grue, to arrive breathless at the smiddy. The garron was waiting patiently, hitched to a ring. Her big sister, Lizzie, was there too, sent to find out what was keeping her. The smith pointed to the sun, beginning to drop and now a fair way north of Menmuir kirk:

'We was stairtin' to think ye was wandert. Did ye see ony tigers?' Maggie was confused and blurted out, best she could

'A saw lots of horses, big, big horses. No like this ane'. She stroked the garron's flank. 'An' there was a cuddy, tae, wi' a meenister mannie'. The smith raised his eyebrows, smiled and asked

'But nae tigers?'

'There wis a knight wi' a sword an' a steel bunnet as said he was a tiger'. The smile fell from the smith's face.

'Thon knight: did he hae a beard? An' did he hae oan a *léine cròchach*?' Maggie did not know the term but it fair described his tunic.

'Aye. So he did'.

'Then ye've seen the real tiger and, I'll warrant, ye're the first for 466 year. Tell yer father there'll be naething tae pay'. Sister Lizzie was dumfoondert.

Maggie began the walk back to Balnamoon, just herself and the garron. Lizzie, it seemed, had matters of her own, very much her own, to attend. At the gushet neuk a road-man had just erected a finger-post up beside the drystane dyke, its three arms pointing away from where the three roads met.

'Fit daes it tell?' Maggie asked. The road-man pointed in turn to each of the three arms:

'Edzell 5¼ miles; Brechin 5¾ miles; Kirriemuir 12¾ miles. Fit why d'ye want tae ken, quine?'

'Sae A ken *nivver* tae gang tae yon airts'. To Maggie, the black hands with pointing fingers were clearly meant as warnings. Even so she needed to go the Brechin road – just for half a mile – if she were to get back to Balnamoon. Then she would take a narrow loan leading straight as a die to nowhere in particular along the west side of the Balnamoon policies, before turning off through Balnamoon Woods to follow the track through the dense trees, to where the MacPhees were camped.

*The track through the dense trees*

It was a year later that the *P. & J.* ran with the headline "The Beast of Balnamoon". In Edinburgh, at the High Court of Justiciary, Lord Tannadice had sentenced one Daniel Alexander Mann to death for the rape and murder of Maggie MacPhee as she walked back from the smiddy. It was Mann that, in the words of Lord Tannadice, was "the Beast of Balnamoon".

*A. 'n' E. & the Auto Died Act*

## XVII

# A. 'n' E. & THE AUTO DIED ACT

They'd met in A. & E.  No-one seemed too badly hurt though all were in some pain.  The two ambulance crews had parked them to one side while attending to the formalities, the bureaucracy that precedes actual admission.  There had been no frantic scrimmages around fast-trundling trolleys; no holding aloft of blood, plasma or saline solution by medical escorts urgently herding through doors held wide into strangely unpopulated corridors; no anxious exchanges of data on the hoof nor fleeting fearful phone calls to expectant surgeons even now struggling into scrubs and checking the edges on new scalpels in their opera theatres of cruelty.  Nor was there a Greek chorus of twelve dreadful-masked nurses chanting

> *Curette and osteotome*
> *Mallet and dilator*
> *Scissors, drill and dermatome*
> *Retractor, elevator*
> *Chisel, lancet, sponge and saw*
> *Mesh and suture ever ... more!*

as, hands linked, they encircled the patient, dancing.  There was no keening of conch, kithara, lyre and aulos; no frame drum syncopation as mænads pranced about the birling bier; no rattle of clappers; and satyrs, if there were any, played secretly their pipes. No, there was a distinct lack of drama.

To say that they had first met in A. & E. is not strictly true; and even there there had been no formal introductions; waiting room etiquette discouraged personal exchanges; no outrageously embosomed matron had circulated among them presenting stranger to stranger or reuniting old acquaintances; there had been no receiving line. Perhaps it was thought that the collision had been presentation enough, though truth be told, such exchanges as there had been at the time had wanted somewhat for conversational refinement.

It wasn't as if either vehicle had been speeding – it wasn't as if either vehicle could speed, given, in both cases, their excess of age and deficiency of power. But the one had gradually caught the other as they trundled along the inside lane and would remain its shadow until such time as a favourable wind, a long downhill stretch and an absence of oncoming traffic might make possible overtaking. No such problems for Larry Hawson's driver, though: his eight-wheel milk-tanker was empty. He'd being blasting towards them when his trailer cast an outer, off-side rear tyre. The tyre had hurtled on, unattached, unimpeded, at 50mph to smash into Rona and Malki's oncoming Mini-van which was instantly shunted by the larger, ex-Royal Mail Bedford van that was Janina's transport – as well as that of her troupe, all of whom lay in a heap in the back, asleep. As they say: it all happened so quickly.

In A. & E. things were not happening quickly; things were proceeding calmly, deliberately, now that initial assessments were complete. Today they would call it "triage", but not in 1970. Back then the word "assessment" was quite good enough, amplified as required by the words "priority" and "order". One by one they were taken off for treatment to re-emerge in "Waiting" later, sometimes much later, variously modified with stookie, surgical collars and less impressive examples of surgical dressing – all apart from Rona, who was being kept in overnight for observation.

Meanwhile, in his elegant Melville Street gallery, Marco de Ricci, one of Leith's finest and *enfant terrible* of Edinburgh's art establishment, was, as ever, revelling in his status and the attention it brought – not least from the several elegant young modistes forever fluttering, forever flattering, forever fawning. His plans for next year's Festival were bearing fruit. Trips to Belgrade and Düsseldorf had secured two artists with whom he would again rattle Edinburgh's cage. He would bring together under one roof Adrijana Milanovič and Josef Schlingel. It was sure to be unmissable – unmissable, that is, by the art establishment, by the nomenklatura of the broadsheets, by the art-camp-followers, the arti-chatterati upon whom success depended. After all, de Ricci's was a commercial gallery for all its cultural pretensions. Not that the gallery itself would be the venue: its position was perhaps a little too off-centre and, in any case, the work of both Milanovič and Schlingel would likely risk its late Georgian elegance and de Ricci's lease. Tucked away in the Old Town, though, and scheduled for demolition, the one-time poor-house, workhouse, drill-hall and armoury would be ideal – once cleared of most of its visible history; even so, the manacles hanging on its diseased walls would stay. They would resonate with both Milanovič and Schlingel.

Those two had never met, despite their links with Flux-US, a New York based, international, interdisciplinary group of artists, composers, designers and poets fixated on process and despising result. It presented itself as "nearly always a discourse on the failure of discourse". De Ricci liked the idea of German Josef, a former member of Nazi Youth, collaborating with Serbian Adrijana whose relatives numbered among the 90,000 killed in the notorious Jasenovak extermination camp, courtesy of the all-too-collaborative Croats. Neither had demurred at the invitation. Now de Ricci was mulling over their proposals – nothing too definitive, but enough for advance publicity. Auto-destructive art was their common theme: in Schlingel's case, objectively so; for Milanovič it would be subjective.

Back in A. & E., eighty miles away, another new alliance was being forged. United in angry contempt of Larry Hawson, his company, his driver and his lorry – but also not unhopeful of considerable compensation (eventually) – they too were discovering much in common. How odd that Janina and her puppeteers should just bump into Malki and Rona, performance-poet and singer-songwriter, like that. It was Janina (maybe still a little concussed) who said

'Perhaps we should try to get something positive out of this – not only compensation.  An act of fate's thrown us together:  so we act upon it.  Literally.  A performance poet, a singer-songwriter and four puppeteers with a van-load of life-size puppets, automata and masks ought, surely, to be able to create something out of this?'

Three months later Janina Kowacz was pitching to Marco de Ricci, initially in Polish (which she knew he understood) and then in English, upon which he complemented her, unaware she'd actually been born and raised in a camp near Banchory, home of the Polish army's exiled Intelligence Battalion.  This was her proposal:

> A 45-minute live performance titled  *A. 'n' E. & the Auto Died Act* with a cast of actors, life-size puppets and automata re-enacting the last days in the life of a VW Beetle called Gregor as it disintegrates on the A. 'n' E. Repair Shop's forecourt patiently enduring intermittent mechanical surgery and awaiting a possible owner transplant……
>
> The cast:
>
> Gregor (a modified Beetle body mounted on a stage truck).
>
> Netta-san, a nun and 6th dan aikidoka.  Gregor's owner.
>
> Formica, a giant tyre ant; the antagonist and cause of Gregor's downfall.

Ivor Bookman, an aspiring, self-taught mechanic whose efforts to save Gregor eventually prove useless.

Mr Tinker, the garagiste.

Mrs Tinker, wife of the above and "no better than she should be".

Constable Haywain, a rural policeman.

Inspector Knox, a rural detective and satyr given to ribaldry.

Inspector Cauls, another detective, something of a head-case.

Father Apophthegmata, a Coptic priest given to pithiness and desert boots.

Chorus of medical disorderlies.

The plot:

a surreal and absurd tragedy in which Gregor's downfall because of the random malice of the giant tyre-ant, Formica, and the subsequent attempts at his rehabilitation by Ivor Bookman, are all ultimately fruitless. A calamitously free-wheeling pastiche of declamatory prose, bawdy haiku, music-hall ballad, mime, masked dance and solo bugle. Janina elaborated, describing an existential black comedy with tragic consequences.

De Ricci signalled silently an acolyte.  She nodded, left and returned with a tray of small cups and a faceted, narrow-waisted, polished, aluminium pot, the epitome of 1930s styling. There arose the bitter, evocative aroma of Italian coffee; it infiltrated; it suffused; it said to Janina that she was not about to be hustled out of the door with solicitous smiles and extravagant expressions of regret.

'Dobry!  Buono!  Good' he said, finally settling on English.  'Run through all of that again'.  She did and de Ricci looked thoughtful for a moment, then said  'I think it needs a dog'.

'A dog?'

'Tak – sì – yes, a dog would be good.  I can see all that you are telling me but I was conscious, increasingly conscious, of something missing, of something needed to make the piece …. coalesce.  It needs a dog'.  Janina was doubtful but pleased that de Ricci seemed already so engaged.

'Any particular kind of dog?'

'It wants to be a quite big dog – not tremendously big, but big, you know?'  He let his hand float just below desk height. 'And with character. Maybe a   '  He struggled for the word he was wanting. 'Yes. I know! A borzoi; a borzoi would be just the thing, just the right dog for the part'.

'A walk-on part, right?'  It had dawned on Janina that borzois are silent so could not be expected to speak.  But, of course, confounding expectations was very much part of the piece.  It had possibilities and with her mixed troupe anything was possible.  'Mmmm' she said 'I rather like that'.  De Ricci refilled her cup.

It was as well, de Ricci reflected, that he did not have to do all the leg-work himself, not any more.  The more disagreeable aspects of mounting exhibitions, Fringe events and such-like could be delegated to Charmion, Melissa, Phœbe or whoever.  Xanthe, it was, drew the really short straw; but if Josef Schlingel required a supply of un-rendered animal fat, then someone had to go the abattoir to make the necessary arrangements; while sourcing 160 ft$^2$ of $\frac{1}{2}$"-thick grey felt at a price that de Ricci thought acceptable was Cecily's challenge.  As for Adrijana Milanovič – well, de Ricci felt it would be best to deal with *her* requirements himself since:  not only would the array of electric heaters contravene all regulations if installed permanently;  the drugs required to induce her voluntary catatonia were not available on prescription.  Only the knives were unproblematic given de Ricci's family catering connections.  But he worried that an Edinburgh audience might be too reticent or feel too sophisticated to intervene before things went too far.  But then, live theatre was always risky; that was its attraction.

There had been ample pre-publicity.  Josef Schlingel had reached Edinburgh via Rotterdam and Hull in his modified Horch, ex-military Heavy Field Car.  He had posed for photographs, leaning against one of its massive mudguards; he wore his trade-mark black sou'wester. There ensued an outbreak

*Schlingel had reached Edinburgh*

of sou'westers among Edinburgh's impressionable. Adrijana Milanovič had been detained by airport security and subjected to searches that most would have found humiliating but which, for her, were enjoyable; and she was only too happy to explain the scars (some quite recent) with which her body was liberally disfigured; but her explanation of auto-destructive art had confused them and they'd contacted traffic police. Adrijana's detention made it on to local news, with just sufficient incoherent detail to titillate.

De Ricci had scheduled Schlingel, Milanovič and *A 'n' E and the Auto Died Act* to be in repertory, the performances alternating. But he'd not reckoned on Burn(e)s: and not just that "The best-laid schemes o' mice an' men/Gang aft agley". To Schlingel the word "goose" had two connotations and he intended subjecting the one to the other, publicly, as part of a piece which, so he maintained, "examined landscape and water management". That the object was passive (being dead) and the assailant very active immediately outraged all and sundry, particularly those who'd not been able to see that part of Schlingel's exhibition before an enforced withdrawal. As for Milanovič, naked and prone in a drug-induced catatonic stupor on a block of ice beneath the array of three-bar electric fires….. the audience participation expected to rescue her had, indeed, not materialised: the unfortunate Milanovič had sustained second degree burns over a third of her body before someone eventually pulled the plug and the still-catatonic Milanovič was hospitalised. To some, that was all part of the performance; others deplored the intervention in what they considered an evolving work of art, art in flux. Milanovič's entire *praxis* (as she called it) was in the realm of auto-destructive art, although she was unusual in being both the artist and, as it were, the canvas.

And what of *A. 'n' E. & the Auto Died Act* ? We shall never know. The venue was peremptorily shut down: a suitably existential ending for what was ultimately a non-existent production.

# XVIII

# GAS

'Why? Why _do_ you always wear that thing? Winter, summer, autumn, spring; fair or foul: every time we meet for a blether, you always wear …. that … cloak? Why?'

Charity was not noted for her understanding. Feeling, for Charity, was something exclusively physical – a tactile activity; consideration was another word for bribe; and sensitivity was something she only ever mentioned to her GP. So Charity tended to blurt. She would, as they say, "come out with things". Where others might advance cautiously into a topic, testing the water with metaphoric toes, Charity blundered blithely, leaving her listeners slaurit with her slaisters of ill-digested opinion and gobbets of bile. Where others might raise a moistened finger (again, metaphorically) to check the strength and direction of the prevailing wind-of-thought (before launching) Charity poked hers in your eye. None of which, however, was deliberate. If Charity had a saving grace, it was her lack of malice; she never intended to hurt people; she just couldn't help herself. She was utterly uninhibited: by which I don't mean her personal behaviour gave cause for reproof or censure, as far as is known (and some things are better not known) but her opinions were not constrained by <u>any</u> awareness of their effect on others.

'Don't you like it?' Persephone was hurt – both by Charity's point-blank question and her own unusually irritable reaction. She should not allow Charity's tactlessness to get to her; after all, she'd known her long enough, so she ought to be used to it. She had been just the same at school. There, Charity's callous indifference had restricted her circle of friends somewhat and Persephone had sometimes regretted her own inclusion. Perhaps she was too kind; perhaps too easy-going; perhaps it was all <u>another</u> aspect of her fate. At school everyone had called her "Seph", which she rather liked and – given her long oval face, ever-so-slightly dark complexion, dark eyes and dark hair – it was not inappropriate. Now, though, Charity had started calling her "Perse" which, with its suggestion of wrinkling parsimony, was unwelcome; more unwelcome still was the thought that some might think it short for Percy – with all that that might conjure. She was thankful no-one else had followed suit (at least, not so far) and, in tutorials she was addressed formally, still, as Miss Perez.

Persephone knew very well why she always wore that cloak; she had her reason, a reason she preferred to keep to herself: for Persephone was conscious of her Kaballah[28]. She smiled inwardly, bitterly, and turned away to gaze through the window at the street below. The others had yet to arrive, so she hoped she might glimpse them coming, unknowing, to her rescue. But the view was restricted: nothing at all could be seen of the pavement beneath, unless one opened the window and craned one's neck; while the other side was far less frequented, being always in shadow and, in any case, lacking anything much of interest. Further along though, where the street curved away in an arc before debouching down into the Grassmarket, there was more to be seen; but Fi and Morag were unlikely to approach from that end, unless they'd risked a stotter down Candlemaker Row – always chancy in the wet. Not that it was raining all that heavily – more of a smirr, but it still made some pavements very greasy. Footsteps on the stair, however, and noisy chatter disrupted Persephone's concern: Fi and Morag had arrived unseen and were even now disturbing the woman in the far corner who was writing obsessively in a lined refill pad, a half-drunk cappuccino ignored and only just out of danger. The two burst across the room in an excess of extended arms and straining haversacks that threatened the imminent loss of all their contents. The barista, half-hidden by the monstrous, stainless steel, two-lever espresso machine shuffled cups and saucers in readiness.

'Oh, thank goodness you've arrived' smiled Persephone. 'Charity has been giving me a hard time'.

'What have I said?' demanded Charity, genuinely puzzled.

'She has taken exception to my poncho'.

'All I wanted to know was why Perse always wears it when we meet up for a news'.

'Why shouldn't she?' (It was Morag.) 'I always wear the same anorak, but you don't ask *me* why'.

'That's different. You've only got the one;  but I happen to know that Perse has any amount of clothes she could wear – instead of this thing'. Charity plucked at the heavy, silver, open-weave silk that fell in generous folds from Persephone's slender shoulders.

'You're only jealous, Charity:  so give over. Tell us all about the exciting world of computer science – what's been happening to you since we last met for a pow-wow?'

It was odd that, after more than two years, the four women continued as they had in first year, the time when they'd all been in hall together. First-year friendships tended to fade away in second year, once students moved on to their specialisms; but though Charity had become one of Professor Michaelson's star students;  and Persephone was now utterly immersed in the Department of European Languages;  and Fiona and Morag were following different courses in the School of Celtic and Scottish Studies;  they still made time in their schedules to meet up twice a term for a gossip – and always here, always in the upstairs room overlooking Victoria Street where, for most of the day, the management was quite relaxed about the speed of one's coffee-drinking. And where, despite the stampeded stair, the shrieking boutades of the Gaggia and the pulses of chatter from other tables, the woman in the far corner always scribbled away, relentlessly.

So their chatter rattled on, incoherently, randomly, instants of serious conversation just as instantly dissolving into insignificant chit-chat; phases of considered deliberation giving rise to anguished heart-to-hearts; tête-à-têtes erupting into general blather; as events both on- and off-campus were aired, shaken out, held up for inspection, comparison and, just occasionally, for advice.

In later years Persephone often marvelled at those afternoons in the upstairs room in Kinnell's. She had long lost touch with the others. Charity's last-known whereabouts had been Cupertino; Fiona had captured an ambitious young naval officer at a ship's dance at Rosyth and must by now have become very "establishment"; and Morag was reputedly living off the land somewhere in Assynt. But for ninety minutes, twice a term, their lives *had* run on the same track, unwary of the points and junctions ahead. Did the others have no foreknowledge of their fates? None of them? Did any of them, any of the other three, look back now at those sessions and marvel, as Persephone was doing, at their ability to: chatter seamlessly about matters both consequential and inconsequential; to natter about nothing; to jaw and to rabbit, to bore and be crabbit, be braw and to gab it; the white and the black, the clype and the craic? And what of that woman who was always there, at the wee corner table, always scribbling away: what, Persephone wondered, had ever become of her? Had she, perhaps, divined something of the answer to Charity's question? She remembered how the woman had started and then stared when Morag wrenched a text book from her bag, *Culhwc ac Olwen*, and pointed to the bit about King Arthur's *llen* or veil. At which, not to be outdone, Fiona had tugged out her copy of the *Mabinogion* to read out a passage about Caswallawn's cloak. And they had both referred to the *Nibelungenlied* and Siegfried's cape. Fiona had joked and said

'But Seph's cape doesn't work, though, does it? We can still see her, thank goodness'. Charity had looked totally baffled.

*A scaled-down, gimcrack San Gimignano*

A warm breeze had got up and the leaves of the surrounding birches rustled. Redstarts and warblers were making themselves busy and, high above, a huge cruising lammergeier shrugged lazily past on a surveillance mission. A green lizard watched her, cheekily, from its sunlit rock. Squint and twisting towers of rough, white, three metre corrugated concrete cubes, crudely fenestrated and separated by projecting floor slabs, were piled one upon another; they teetered haphazardly above the young trees[29]. It was like a scaled-down, gimcrack San Gimignano reimagined by a madman. Beside her, irregular white steps wound down into the grey, gritty earth; each turn marked by a grey lead monolith to lead towards the labyrinth.

Persephone bent, cloaked in nothing save the heavy, silver, open-weave silk that had defied and offended Charity. With a single stroke she lit the propane torch lying upwards between her naked feet. The time had come, at last, to illuminate the meaning of her mantle – her gas mantle.

*The exuberant girls were first to arrive*

## IXX

# LETTUCE  KNIVES

It had become a matter of grave public concern.  Police and courts alike were struggling to cope with the ever-increasing prevalence of knife crime, of the apparent need for young people, especially, to arm themselves with cold, sharpened steel. Restrictions on sales brought little by way of evident improvement; on-line retailers in particular seemed adept at evading attempted proscription.  Calls from sundry pulpits to remove the points from all knives offered for sale were met with derision in the catering industry and from elderly, gnarled cutlers in Sheffield whose hand-made penknives were collectors' treasures.  Death and permanent disfigurement stalked the land; mutilation had become a way of life both dealt out and, in some quarters, seemingly accepted.  In desperation, the government decreed the need for a "celebrity" to front a new campaign, someone admired by the "demographic" it wanted to reach:  so it appointed a "knife tsar" or, more accurately, a "knife tsarina". Winner of a "reality" tv show; whose name appeared above an agony daughter column (she was still only 16) in an on-line fanzine called Sticky.wot; with an alleged following on Twitter of more than a million; her own sandwich and wrap channel on YouTube; a fashion tv channel expected shortly; and her band PnukPnust scheduled to headline at Glastonbury. Meanwhile, she never appeared anywhere now without her lettuce knife – for, it had been argued that, as she had become what was now termed an "influencer", lettuce knives would become the latest "must-have". If there was any cynicism underlying that assertion, it was soon dispelled – or, rather, the cynicism that underpins all marketing was once again proved not misplaced. Within weeks, youths totally unfamiliar with salad or any of its features (direct or indirect) were parading their lettuce knives; in the sweat-shops of Hong Kong and Singapore, not only were all manner of lettuce knife and lettuce knife variants being hustled to market, so too were the oh-so-necessary accessories – sheaths, covers and holsters, possessing all manner of attributes: shockproof, waterproof, scratch-proof, scan-proof, monogrammed, anti-magnetic, leather, p.v.c., rubber, self-cleaning, dish-washer-proof, embroidered. They could be had as appendages to trouser belts; as clip-ons to top pockets; they could be strapped to thighs, calves, ankles, forearms and even bosoms; and, for export to the Tyrol, they could be attached to hatbands.

Not that the aggression stopped; but those subjected to lettuce knife attacks seldom bothered A & E: attempts at stabbing were literally pointless since lettuce knives bend on impact; and an attempted slashing would result in nothing worse than a slight graze – which, of course, did not even turn brown.

But, for the girls of the St Aloysius Convent School the lettuce knife revolution did not go far enough. It was Bridget who started it. She'd made her Friday evening confession and was sure she'd heard Fr Dermot mumble through the grille "Lettuce pray and lettuce give thanks…" Bridget needed to hear no more. She knew she had been granted a revelation. She knew she had been given a mission and, as a missionary, she had first to inspire a devoted band of followers with whom she could go forth and spread the word – that word being that "lettuction" (as it had been formally labelled) that "lettuction" had not gone far enough; it was insufficiently radical. They, the girls of St Aloysius, had to go further. An act of faith was ordained. A fortnight later Bridget and her small band of acolytes issued their challenge to the boys of King William's. The girls determined the place; the boys chose the date, April 11th. In suitably tie-dyed t-shirts and lacrosse goggles, the exuberant girls were first to arrive; but of the boys, there was no sign. The girls fingered their lettuce knives, the lettuce knives that had cost them so much effort, required so much skill, the lettuce knives that were one hundred percent pure lettuce, but hardened in the freezer overnight and burnished with multiple layers of hair lacquer.

They waited, but pointlessly. The Billies had not shown. The girls headed back through the woods, along the path that led to the road, disappointed and yet buoyed by conviction, by faith in the unassailable "correctness" of their stance: that might is not always right – except, as it shortly transpired, when

*153*

ambushed by a gang of boys, each one wielding an enormous cos.

For the boys, afterwards, there was the added, ironic satisfaction of having seen off the girls of St Aloysius with romaines. Their leader, Dominic (who had latterly taken to calling himself Min) then led his gang in the ritual consumption of their lactucal weaponry – but without dressing, of course. Theirs, he told them, had been a victory in a "Cos célèbre". They had triumphed over what he called "the lettuce naïves".

## XX

# THE RIVER

The river lay ahead, invisible, but we knew it was there. The map – with its grotesque filigree of distorted brown whorls randomly transgressed by filaments of red, black, orange and blue plus its surcharged litter of a typographic omnium gatherum only partly intelligible – told us that much; and, in any case, given the lie of the land, it had to be so. Grasping our sticks, we turned left off the metalled road at a point where it had begun to dip and to swerve down into an umbrageous cloister of trees – oaks, beeches, elms – to be lost from view in their dense shadow. The mountains beyond, across the unseen valley, were glimpsed only momentarily beneath a wedge of bleached sky and then hidden by that voluptuous canopy. Our side-lane was both rough and grassy, sunken between two high brambly banks with two deeply-gouged ruts made by the yellow lorries that intermittently drove towards us and forced us up on to those banks where dog-roses grew and from which exploded the occasional surprised mole. We tramped on, the track gradually descending, dimly conscious of the time and becoming dimly conscious too of the gradual erasure of most of the landscape, its features melting away, as if its map were being blanched; for, as we advanced, the panorama's detail correspondingly retreated, or elided, until almost nothing distinctive remained. In what had now subsided into a landscape virtually featureless only two trees still stood out. Side by side they towered over the lane, their massive, deep-fissured trunks and branches contorting and entwining far above our heads so that, from certain angles, they appeared almost architectural, as if metamorphosing into aerial buildings, buildings in part skeletal, anarchic, organic structures and as if they themselves were their own scaffolding. In their tattered baldacchino could be seen some half dozen, large, straggly, unoccupied nests of untidy sticks, honeycombed with sky. So fantastic were the trees that we risked being too late by stopping to photograph their writhing, grappling limbs: first as we approached; next from below; and then looking back, even returning, running, to take further shots, before finally hurrying on until we reached, in awful contrast, a heavy, rectangular-mesh perimeter fence, taut between tall, forked stanchions of reinforced-concrete, wreathed with razor wire, that had arisen, humming, on our left; beyond it, a fighter jet took off.

The lane widened, becoming gravelly, less rutted; and we hastened to pass a balding, bearded, middle-aged man His white shirt, khaki chinos constructed of pockets, his pair of trekking sticks and the binoculars in their brown leather case slung from his neck, seemed to define him as a tourist; but you could never be sure.

The airfield gave way to railway sidings, beyond which our immediate goal could now be seen.

'It leaves at five' you said.

The station itself was far from imposing. It was no monument to nineteenth-century railway megalomania; no grandiose hotel fronted it; no soaring flights of cast iron and glass sheltered either trains or their passengers; nor did it evoke any sense of an era bygone, nor of its being a gateway to exotic destinations. It was, in every sense, a terminus; and, being a terminus, relatively few were they who left. Rather, it sprawled confusedly as if built at intervals and without any great regard for unity or cohesion. More crematorium than cathedral: pale, blue-grey-painted brick walls and low, glazed, grimed canopies encased a broad, zig-zag corridor that did duty as a concourse. Soiled acoustic tiles drooped askew from the ceiling grid and baleful fluorescent lights flickered erratically. Identical display cases fixed, irregularly, to the walls contained a permanent exhibition of blank timetables alternating with reproductions of paintings (Bosch, Zdzisław Beksiński, Fuseli, Anastasia Plüch, Escher) each picture distorted and re-proportioned so as to fit its frame. Sleeping curators, hunched on camp-stools, chins on sticks, guarded the access to each platform.

'It's number one' you said as we ran beneath a suspended "15".

We already had our tickets, though they were different. The machine on the wall accepted yours: two-coloured, stiff,

157

with rounded corners, the size of a credit card. Mine – long, narrow and typewritten on grey sugar paper – it rejected. At the barrier you were waved through; I was stopped while the collector examined a handwritten, foolscap sheet.

'That is good' she told me, in an accent impossible to place, 'here your name is. Just allow me the print of your thumb so you can pass'. She presented an ink-pad and I duly left a red impression beside my name on a list that contained no other names.

It was already past five yet the train still stood at the platform having, it seemed, been late arriving consequent, it was said, to a diversion. Passengers were being urged to hurry. In the confusion there was no sign of you and I supposed you to have already boarded. Moving through the coaches I searched in vain and, as I did, the train started. I hurried back, meaning to jump down into the retreating station where I imagined you, in turn, to be searching for me, fruitlessly. As I wrestled with the door, the guard's hand closed on mine.

'Don't do it' she said, perhaps misunderstanding my intentions, then added 'Look again. She will be somewhere'.

I nosed forwards once more, incessantly, laboriously, timelessly through a sequence of ill-assorted carriages furnished with tables and chairs of every description, haphazard about a meandering central gangway. Larger tables were set for dinner with heavy silver cutlery and plates bearing the railway company's monogram; others, being smaller, had vases of black wax flowers – tulips and roses. Older people relaxed in striped deckchairs. Children were excited and scrambled in the netting of the luggage racks, hiding behind portmanteaux, toppling valises and bestriding Gladstone bags. I looked intently at every passenger, searching for your face, willing you to be found, patiently waiting – as indeed you were, at last, at the very front.

'Where were you?' you asked, as with screeching wheels, the train veered sharply left and into a long, rusted, ramshackle, corrugated-steel structure – where it stopped.

'It looks like we too have been diverted' someone said.

'Speak for yourself' snapped a bearded man with frame-less glasses who had been engrossed in a cryptic cross-word.

No-one moved, wondering what was to happen. Lights in the carriage had gone out. In the gloom of the confining shed little could be discerned, its corroded walls rendered darkest black in contrast to the blinding spatter of light that forced itself through the scabs of decay. Shortly, our engine steamed past the window, heading for the other end. A shudder: and we assumed it had re-coupled. You and I were now at the back. Its wheels again screeching, the train moved once more, as it was pulled back out into the light, veering hard left and moving very slowly, so very slowly, as the track started abruptly to ascend, remorselessly. Its climb was agonising, interminable, seeming at times barely to be moving at all.

'I think it needs a push' you said.

*The viaduct*

We climbed down from the rear step – you, me and Anubis, your Ibizan hound. The track had become rack-and-pinion and much narrower than before; the train itself seemed to have slimmed accordingly. The three rails were now rising even more steeply, tortuously, and the train laboured at walking pace its pistons chittering with a frenzy not reflected in the train's grinding momentum. Pushing made no apparent difference but at least, so we imagined, the engine had marginally less to do while we walked behind. An ill-maintained wooden post-and-wire fence flanked the line as if to prevent its recoil and escape to easier terrain and causing dog-walkers to squash themselves flat to let the train struggle past. High above us, ahead, we got our first glimpse of the white, granite viaduct – a series of semi-circular arches on a procession of narrow piers that grew ever taller as they stepped out across a deep, rocky gorge. It resembled a huge Roman aqueduct but constructed in just a single stage, not two or three tiers, rising out of the abyss from which also arose the roar of furious water.

'I've always wanted to cross that' I said, although I knew I'd never seen it before.

The train paused to catch its breath and we struck out on our own, ahead of it, glad of our sticks, striding from sleeper to sleeper, crunching on the white, rocky ballast, glancing back occasionally to make sure we were not about to be overtaken. Only when its shrill whistle proclaimed its renewed ascent did we stop to find a point from which we might easily rejoin without its needing to pause. But by then we had reached the viaduct's abutment.  A small group of grey seals lay sunbathing on the track and, at our approach, their pups took fright, squirmed to the edge of the low parapet to hurl themselves down, down .... into the unseen river.

# XXI

# JAM

She was the last.  She announced

'It's called *A Damsonnet'*.  She did not explain.  Unlike those who'd spoken before her, she held not a book but a single sheet of lined paper from which she read:

### *A Damsonnet*

*Where once the hedgerows bound the pastures tight*
*And circumscribed the ruminating kye*
*(Whose leathern flanks their tenderness belie)*
*Debarred by dense entangled thorns from flight:*
*Now are those margins scarred by axe and blight.*
*In headway's name the landscape abnegates*
*Those hedgerows greedy farmers desecrate*
*With torch, with bill-hook, slasher, dynamite.*
*Aye, devastating force of ev'ry kind*
*Is waged against those banks that guard and store,*
*That guard our beasts and store fruits unconfined*
*By horticulture or by orchard lore*
*Lost hips, lost haws, lost sloes, lost brammles; damsons*
*too, once fav'rite fruit for rustic jams*.

She went back to her place.

'Why is that poem your favourite, Anna?' The teacher's voice was soft; it was not a challenge.

'It's because …. my father wrote it'.

As the children filed out at lowsing-time, the teacher put her hand on Anna's shoulder.

'Has still no news arrived?' she asked. Anna shook her head and went to gather up her young brothers and sister for their long walk back up the valley to the farm. She had much to do. With all the men, apart from her ancient great-grandfather, having volunteered or else been conscripted, it fell to the women to undertake everything needed to keep the farm from total dereliction – though it had scarcely kept them alive, ever; theirs was a subsistence. It would have been easier if her grandfather, who was still pretty fit, hadn't volunteered as an anti-aircraft

artillery-man, over in the next valley, up at the reservoir; but his past experience would be invaluable. As yet no refugees nor "dafties" had been billeted upon them, but her mother feared it could happen; extra hands might be useful (though extra food would be hard to come by) as would additional income. Only the black-market sale of milk, eggs, piglets and bull calves brought in any cash, and little enough of that. But although the life was hard, the relentless labour gruelling, Anna knew that theirs was a better life right now than that of those living in the cities, those toiling in munitions factories, those in darkness down the mines. At least Anna and her family had better access to fresh food, were less dependent on ration book coupons and, on their remote hillside, were hardly likely to be the target of bombers. But not so, the reservoir. Were that to be breached the resulting deluge would engulf all the villages and towns further down the next valley – and all the people in them. So her mother's father, whose farm it was, spent much of his time manning an anti-aircraft gun, away over the hills, returning perhaps just once a week to check that things at home had not gone wholly to wrack and to ruin and to talk to his belovéd bees. He held firmly to the tradition that bees must be told everything – not merely of births, deaths and marriages, but of all events touching upon the farm and those who lived and worked there. Her mother said that the hives were Grandpa's confessional – but did not doubt the observance would endure even when Grandpa was gone.

As for Anna's father: he had been an incomer, a townie, originally, who had embraced both Anna's mother and the hard manual labour of marginal farming while continuing to write for various periodicals and journals. He had gone off to war only with the greatest reluctance, a conscript, bitterly contemptuous of the jingoistic rhetoric in which "serving one's country" was decorated, deeply sceptical about the motives of those who most loudly promoted conflict, a man without hatred, without any supernatural belief, a man who had come to love *the* country (rather than *his* country) – wherever he encountered it. It had been more than a year since anything had been heard either of or from him. But he came to Anna every day. As she led the kye into the byre for their milking; as she tucked up her plets under her white screen, as she sted her crackie and pail, first at one coo then the next, each with its tail hitched temporar to its right hint-leg, as she fingert their edders, as she tipped the milk from pail to cog and from cog to kirn; as she watched her two young brothers hurl their bogie with its three, small, five gallon kirns doon tae the road-end to wait on the dairy-mannie's horse an' cairt….

Sometimes Anna would just stand in the wee room off the stair where her father used to do his writing. The table beneath the window, the window that looked down over the in-fields, was still strewn with his papers and his notebooks; underneath, concertina files performed document storage duty; the shelf to the left held only his reference books, for the bulk of his library encased the parlour wall; and in a chipped dish stood a large bottle of ink, its cap now somewhat crusted, and beside it a dried-up fountain pen. At the table's centre there hunched a locked, moulded wooden box, floridly emblazoned with the word "Olympia"; it shrouded her father's treasured typewriter. Anna knew where the box's two keys hid. Sometimes she would release the machine from its captivity just to gaze at its dumpy, black-japanned steel carcass crowned by its chromium carriage, extending, offering its battery of fifty lettered buttons, and remember her father typing out final copies for her to carry down to the post office.

Today she was carrying a large basket and an ash crook but, rather than shepherding her young brothers and sister down towards the village, she was rambling the margins of the fields and woods up above the farm. Her father's poem, the one she had read in school yesterday, Friday, arose vividly in her thoughts. Here, still, "hedgerows bound the pastures tight"; no "margins scarred by axe [or] blight" defaced the land farmed by her family. Maybe the hedges did straggle; maybe they did appear wild and unkempt; maybe they did encroach more than was strictly necessary to corral the cattle and to afford them shelter; but they were also home to all manner of bird, beast and beastie. And in amongst the rambling tangle were to be found the hips, the haws, the sloes, the brambles and the damsons lamented by her father; aye, and crab apples too. All the ingredients, in fact, for what her mother called "hedgerow jam" – all, that is, apart from sugar. You could pick all the wild fruit in the world, but without roughly as much sugar there could be no jam-making – and sugar was very strictly rationed. However, there were the bees and the bees made honey which, in turn, could be used to replace sugar – even if the jam did turn out somewhat soft and runny. No matter: it tasted good.

Anna worked her way steadily along the margins, teetering on edges of ditches, reaching, forever reaching, up and over with her crook to bring promising fruit to hand. Little by little her basket filled. She made no attempt to separate the damsons from the sloes, the hips from the haws, the brambles from the crab apples. If that were to happen it could wait until she got back – a good task for her wee sister. Anyway, it would be for her mother to decide: would there be enough of any particular fruit for a pure, single-variety jam? Or, as was usually the case, would all the resulting pots be filled with what her father had dubbed "Mama's Mixtie-Maxtie Mélange"? If only he could come back: to be able to enjoy it, as before, slaithered ower a tattie bannock.

Anna turned for home, her basket brimming; the air had suddenly chilled. She had been so absorbed in foraging she had barely registered the gradual darkening of the autumn sky. She needed back for the evening milking. Heavy clouds were massing to the west. She must hurry if she were not to get a soaking. The wind was rising, funnelling down through a gap in the hills, roaring distantly, somehow…. differently. Just briefly it carried another sound: hollow, rattling, staccato. Anna stopped in her running, stumbling descent and rested on her crook to look back towards the source of that faint, brief, stuttering sound, the sound that had rapidly become a whining, whistling, coffee-grinding, threshing noise that was intensifying fast. The huge, deafening plane, painted in broad waves of green and brown – a long cylinder with a gaping belly beneath vast wings from which projected four engines, two propellers still spinning, its tail ablaze from just behind the concentric red, white and blue circles painted on its side – was barely skimming the tree tops as it staggered erratically down the valley. Moments later: a dull "crump" and a column of smoke and flame told a cowering Anna that there would be no jam.

*He must have lain there all night*

## XXII

# EO ATROX SUM

He must have lain there all night.  His end had been excruciating, evidently.  Even now, his violently contorted corpse stared sightlessly at his coat of arms carved in the sandstone slab, scarcely a decade before, above the door that led to the turret stair.  Perhaps, had he been discovered earlier, he might have survived – assuming that the cause of his collapse had been recognised and an appropriate antivenin been available; not something to be found in Boots.  Scene-of-crime officers were being understandably cautious.  That the vivarium's security had been breached was obvious; but the legally-required list on the vivarium wall gave no clue as to what had actually escaped.  Until a herpetologist could be found to compare the list against those that remained, they were taking no chances.  They noted, however, the empty brandy bottle half-concealed beneath the body and also Lady Breichhame's ungracious parting note transfixed to the kitchen mantle-shelf.

Ten years back such an outcome would hardly have been anticipated. The PM needed a new Advocate General for Scotland following both the party's total eclipse there – and the quiet demission of the previous holder. The field was limited and it was not without misgivings that the high office was awarded to Michaelmas Weanshaw QC, who had just lost the seat of Armagate, Bathburn & Whitdale. A life peerage would, of course, accompany the appointment, the full implications of which were not, to the PM, immediately apparent.

Two months later and four hundred miles to the north, Lord Weanshaw of Breichhame, as he was now styled, leaned on the balcony of the Newts Club (founded 1786), looking down on Princes Street and also on those who, even at that late hour, still thronged the pavement beneath. His celebratory "bash" was going well; the admittance of ladies for the evening had no doubt tempered things somewhat so that, all being well, the young Earl of Glandoghet would think better of his unspeakable party-piece with a pineapple. Even now, Lady Weanshaw was doing her best to dissuade him.

Michaelmas Weanshaw, Scotland's newly-appointed Lord Advocate, let his gaze drift across the gardens, opposite, to the flood-lit castle. His own Castle Breichhame did not rise dramatically from a 250-foot dolerite crag, nor cloak itself in a semi-circular battery; indeed, as yet, it was little more than the ravaged seventeenth-century shell he'd bought cheaply but was about to restore – with the help of more of his wife's wealth. Dixie-Rose O'Shaughnessy Steinmuller, now proudly Lady Weanshaw of Breichhame, would surely wheedle more out of "Daddy" (known still as "The Kerosene King") provided he could be kept sedated and but-dimly aware of his nurses. So far, only the roof had been replaced; but Michaelmas Weanshaw could picture the eventual result of his architect's proposals. He relished the prospect of the great hall, the minstrel's gallery, the wheel stair, the secret intra-mural stair leading to his *Cabinet de Curiosités*, the "Laird's Chaumer", the turret stair, the stone-vaulted sauna and, particularly, the vivarium in the former oubliette. Historic Scotland had drooled over the drawings and Building Control had been easily persuaded that certain elements of the existing Scottish Building Standards were inappropriate in the circumstances. Weanshaw had every confidence in his architect – they'd been at school together and had been in touch ever since: Sir Jamie Cutler-Gullane, only child of Rear Admiral Duthie Cutler-Gullane VC and the Hon. Phœbe Cutler-Cutler-Cutler-Burnes, fifth and final daughter of the Marquess of Clart (a marquessate hence extinguished).

A quarter-mile away, deep in the labyrinth of New Register House, the Lennox Pursuivant of Arms was hard at work – two words not commonly associated either in or with the court of the Lord Lyon. But Lennox (only ever known as Lennox) being also the official Herald Painter was determined to resolve the question of an apt coat of arms for Michaelmas Weanshaw, now Lord Weanshaw of Breichhame. The problem was pressing; the problem was personal – deeply so – and went back many years. Lennox doubted Weanshaw would have any recollection of the particular event. Why should he? In the interval much would have happened, many such episodes (if one is being euphemistic) would have been enacted. The cast list was likely endless. But nothing ever stuck. Such were Weanshaw's connections, so numerous his ties, so weighty the debts owed him: that he seemed to enjoy unlimited credit even if, as Lennox knew, undeservedly. Revenge, it's said, is a dish best eaten cold; but, Tallyrand (or whoever) could not have anticipated the microwave; so things can be re-heated. Lennox, for so long the waiter would now wait upon Weanshaw, that strutting, snorting, flamboyant dandy and serve him a dish truly flambé. Lennox stared at the photograph on the table, a close-up of *Crotalus atrox*, the diamond-back rattlesnake. Among other things, Weanshaw was (Lennox knew) an ophiologist – he both studied and collected snakes; and as a top lawyer he himself was surely juridically serpentine. How would it be if that, somehow, could be used heraldically? Lennox toyed with the phrase "scales of justice".

Back at the Newts Club the celebrations were winding down. The young Earl of Glandoghet had been diplomatically dissuaded from his anánasal party-piece and had gone off in a strunt, though accompanied by Lady Weanshaw seeking to provide easement. Michaelmas, still gazing across at the castle, felt a brief, affectionate caress on his cheek, clad in the tartan he himself had designed blending magenta, twilight lavender and

Mughal green with intermittent threads of red-ochre and black. A ten-button, high-necked, double-breasted, plum-coloured velvet smoking jacket over a violet silk stock secured by an amethyst, completed his evening-wear. Despite the cigar smoke, he recognised the Cologne and had no need to turn. He could feel Jamie Cutler-Gullane's excitement, as he said

'The tenders are all to hand, now. I think I know who we should appoint'.

Later, having bade the last of his guests good-night, Michaelmas took a cab the one-third mile up The Mound to the Lawnmarket whence he disappeared into the shadows of Wardrop's Court before working his way through into Lady Stair's Close and thus to the *pied à terre*, high above, of Sir Jamie Cutler-Gullane. He would be expected.

Over breakfast, their talk was all about Castle Breichhame and its surroundings. The environs of Bathgate are not, exactly, Highland Perthshire; nor was the proximity of a chicken farm and its attendant processing facilities anything to boast about at game fairs; as for the mountainous, pink bings …. well, Michaelmas Weanshaw, lord Weanshaw of Breichhame, did have ideas about those. He'd been excited in a Munich night-club by one Wyatt van Druyer who was, he claimed, "into non-transportable social sculpture and dis-location site denial". For Weanshaw that meant that, with a change in nomenclature and some amendments by a JCB, the bings could become "land art". The bings' actual owners were enthusiastic: an industrial albatross could become an attraction; and they themselves would be transformed into art patrons, having provided aspiring land-artists with a lifetime opportunity and funding bodies with a vehicle for their vision (and the private derision of those same owners). It was what was trendily known as "Disturbing Art". Yet, effortlessly, Castle Breichhame would be relocated out of a post-industrial wasteland and into a sculpture park.

Elisabeth Dinnis was always known as Libby, unfortunately, thus acquiring a punning aptronym that became, indeed, a true example of nominative determinism. She had once been expected to marry Odo von Gotha-Schwartz, Graf in den Schweineställen, but that had proved to be an eruptive relationship that ended explosively in dolorous Accrington. Later she became the wife but, soon, relict of the Rev. Dr Æneas Hands, Dean of St Mary's, whose preferment and early demise were neither ever satisfactorily explained. Thus Libby was now reduced to haunting the aisles, not of the cathedral but of Marks and Spencer's food hall, in the hope of chance encounters. Lennox, clutching a lunch-time sandwich and swithering between the "Less Than 5" queue and the bewildering self-service check-out, had been easy prey.

Libby's Dublin Street flat had been no great detour for Lennox and, matters having gone well that morning, there was no hurry to get back to New Register House. And matters were about to get very much better, once Libby had recovered from a quite unanticipated discovery. Later, it unfolded that both Libby and Lennox had knowledge of Michaelmas: information that would find no place in a liturgical calendar and which would certainly burnish none of Weanshaw's credentials: information shared – and not only with a bottle and a half of M. & S. claret. After that, there was certainly no imperative for Lennox to get immediately back to work.  Libby's testimony had clinched things.  Lennox now knew not only what Weanshaw's coat of arms would look like, but also the wording of the integral motto – for in Scotland, uniquely, the motto is an actual component of the grant of arms both graphically and verbally and, as such, cannot be changed.

How Weanshaw had glowed when presented with the completed achievement.  There had been a small ceremony in the Signet Library to which the upper echelons of Edinburgh's legal fraternity had been invited.  It was Lennox who solemnly unveiled the official blazon.  There had been polite applause and a quick return to the charms of the '47 Château Cheval Blanc. Just two of the older men, whose Latin extended beyond such legal terms as *Ad factum praestandum, De jure, Ex parte, Ipso facto, Loco parentis,* and suchlike, debated the motto.

'How, I wonder' mused one 'does Weanshaw interpret that?'  Any response was forestalled by Weanshaw himself, who had eavesdropped.

'Lennox, there, assures me it signifies "In this am I terrifying" and I cannot disagree with such a distinguished Pursuivant of Arms as Lennox or, indeed, the sentiment'.

'Ah, yes – that it may' muttered one of the two scrutineers, at that moment catching Lennox's eye, knowingly. Perhaps, thought Lennox, the man had suspected the other, covert interpretation, though not, probably, its reason:

*Eo atrox sum* – I'm terrible, at that.

## XXIII

# DON'T TALK ABOUT IT

## A PLAY FOR TWO VOICES, IN ONE ACT

*DRAMATIS PERSONÆ:*

Q　　*Someone who asks questions. High-pitched nasal voice.*

Pat.　*Somewhat truculent & increasingly nervous.*

*SCENE:　A bare, windowless room with a table and 2 chairs*

**Q**　　They certainly did you proud, don't you think?

**Pat.**　If you say so.

**Q**　　Don't you think they've done you proud?

**Pat.**　Well.  It's hard to say.

**Q**　　Really?  Why do you say that?

**Pat.**　It's the first.

**Q**　　And that makes it difficult?

**Pat.**　I've nothing to compare it with.

**Q**　　Nothing of your own, do you mean?

**Pat.**　Yes.

**Q**　　But you'd surely agree it looks very handsome?

**Pat.**   That, actually, is a problem.

**Q**   Would you not want it to look handsome?

**Pat.**   I certainly wouldn't want it to look tatty.

**Q**   Well then?  Where's the problem?

**Pat.**   Of course, you wouldn't _expect_ them to put out something that's tatty.

**Q**   Is there any reason why they might?

**Pat.**   No _reason_, no.

**Q**   Are you saying they might do it thoughtlessly?

**Pat.**   Not at all.  It might be done deliberately.

**Q**   If deliberately there would be a reason, surely?

**Pat.**   _They_ might think so.

**Q**   Are you saying their reason would be spurious?

**Pat.**   Not in their minds, perhaps.

**Q**   But the issue doesn't arise, does it?

**Pat.**   Maybe not, not in this specific case.

**Q**   So, if not in this specific case, where?

**Pat.**   It's a general thing.

**Q**   So what is it you consider to be "general"?

**Pat.**   The relationship.

**Q**   As in the example we have before us?

**Pat.**   No, that's the point.

**Q**   The point being?

**Pat.**   Why is this not an example?

**Q**   You are asking me?

**Pat.**   Maybe you have the answer.

**Q**   As I asked before:  where's the problem in this not being, as you put it, tatty?

AMANDINE GUISE

**Pat.** The fact that it's the very opposite of tatty makes it a distortion.

**Q** I'll grant you it's glossy. But how is that a distortion?

**Pat.** It elevates it, exalts it, and it becomes a surrogate.

**Q** Surrogate... perhaps, but not a replacement, surely?

**Pat.** No, because it changes and distorts scale, for one thing.

**Q** And other things?

**Pat.** Colour....

**Q** And?

**Pat.** Immediacy, intimacy, the whole <u>actual</u> experience.

**Q** And you think all these qualities are distorted by glossiness?

**Pat.** It misrepresents them. It's like dressing up.

**Q** You don't approve of dressing up?

**Pat.** It's all for show.

**Q** Show? Isn't *that* how this all started? Wasn't *that* the original purpose?

**Pat.** And <u>*that*</u> should have been the culmination too. Not <u>*this*</u> thing.

**Q** Mmmmm. Why, I wonder, did you choose that particular word – culmination?

**Pat.** It just came into my head.

**Q** So you didn't choose it, it chose you: is that what you are saying?

**Pat.** If you like.

**Q** But what is it, if I might press you, that *you* like?

**Pat.** What I *would* like would be an end to these questions.

*181*

**Q**    Why is that?

**Pat.**    I don't know why I'm here. I don't know why you are questioning me.

**Q**    Are you expecting or hoping for – to use your word – a culmination?

**Pat.**    I'd like this to be over. I have other things to do.

**Q**    Things you wish to culminate?

**Pat.**    I do have deadlines.

**Q**    Deadlines? Deadlines? Really? Not, perhaps, targets?

**Pat.**    There are dates by which I need to have things done.

**Q**    But not targets ... deadlines?

**Pat.**    They're the same. "Deadlines" was the word that came into my head.

**Q**    So, again, you didn't choose it, it chose you: is that what you're telling me?

**Pat.**    You don't *debate* with yourself, you don't de<u>lib</u>erate which words to use, not when talking.

**Q**    Isn't that risky?

**Pat.**    I mean you don't do it consciously.

**Q**    If you'd chosen consciously, deliberately, might you perhaps have used another word?

**Pat.**    You've already suggested "target".

**Q**    We'll come back to "target". Can I urge you to say more about "culmination"?

**Pat.**    Culmination seems as good a word as any.

**Q**    For <u>any</u> other word?

**Pat.**    For what I was wanting to say!

**Q**   You wouldn't have swapped it, say, for "conclusion"?

**Pat.**   No.  That suggests something slightly different.

**Q**   How about: "climax"?

**Pat.**   So does that. "Climax" also suggests something else.

**Q**   But, even so, would it not be appropriate?

**Pat.**   Sorry, you've lost me.  Semantics are not my thing.

**Q**   If not semantics, what, then, *is* your "thing"?

**Pat.**   That must be obvious.  The evidence is here on the table in front of us.

**Q**   But is it?

**Pat.**   Of course it is.

**Q**   But didn't you characterise it earlier as "spurious"?

**Pat.**   I simply meant that this in itself is not the *real* thing.

**Q**   Would you perhaps concede that it is, even so, evidence of the real thing?

**Pat.**   I suppose it purports to be.

**Q**   And is it not also evidence of something else?

**Pat.**   I don't know what you're getting at.

**Q**   Don't you?

**Pat.**   No.  You talk in riddles. I think you're trying to trap me.

**Q**   Why should I want to do that?

**Pat.**   It's what *you* people do.

**Q**   And who might "we people" be, do you suppose?

**Pat.**   I'm not so stupid as to answer that.

**Q**   Do you think you know the answer?

**Pat.**   The fact that I'm here, in this particular room, is somewhat suggestive.

**Q**    If we'd picked somewhere else, would it have made any difference?

**Pat.**    I suppose it might.  It would depend on where it was.

**Q**    So the <u>context</u> of this discussion matters to you?

**Pat.**    The physical context, yes – the academic too, if you want to call it that.

**Q**    So where, *if* I might prompt you, would you have preferred?

**Pat.**    That, surely <u>is</u> academic – I don't appear to have had any choice.

**Q**    Indulge me.  Suppose you had had a choice?  Where would it have been?

**Pat.**    Nowhere.  I did not ask for this … meeting.

**Q**    Perhaps not, but it was, I fear, inevitable.  So let me press you: where, ideally?

**Pat.**    Not in this cramped, stuffy room, that's for sure.

**Q**    Would I be right in supposing you'd have been happier out-of-doors?

**Pat.**    That's where I'm generally happiest.

**Q**    Indeed, as the evidence before us (spurious or not) demonstrates, surely?

**Pat.**    Obviously.

**Q**    Obviously?  I don't think so or, at least, not entirely. Because which is it: the fresh air or what you do in it that is obvious?

**Pat.**    They can't be separated.

**Q**    I'll grant the *execution* of one depends on the other. But what of motive?

**Pat.** Motive! You make it sound like a crime.

**Q** Who's to say?

**Pat.** What I do is no crime, for heaven's sake.

**Q** Are you sure about that?

**Pat.** If it were there'd be thousands more equally guilty, living and dead.

**Q** Dead?

**Pat.** For heaven's sake, I'm not the first. I'm just one in untold generations.

**Q** Untold? Another interesting choice of words. What is it that's not told?

**Pat.** You're twisting what I say. All I meant was "numberless".

**Q** But *you* are not about "numberless" yourself, are you?

**Pat.** Sorry. You've got me there.

**Q** Absence of numbers is hardly a feature of your work, would you say?

**Pat.** Editions have to be numbered, certainly.

**Q** Do they?

**Pat.** If they are to have any value to collectors, yes.

**Q** So number-less equals worth-less, is that what you are saying?

**Pat.** There's no _ex_trinsic value if by numberless one means innumerable.

**Q** And what of the _in_trinsic value?

**Pat.** That's proportional to scarcity.

**Q** Scarcity? Only scarcity?

**Pat.** At a base, commercial level, yes.

**Q**    What other, higher, level do you have in mind?

**Pat.**    Connoisseurship.

**Q**    And what does connoisseurship comprise?

**Pat.**    Appreciation of aesthetics… ability … provenance.

**Q**    Provenance? That too I find very interesting.  Do I take it you mean its own history?

**Pat.**    That's what is normally meant.

**Q**    The piece's own …. background?

**Pat.**    Yes.  Where it came from, where it has been.

**Q**    As an object?

**Pat.**    As an object, yes.

**Q**    But what about, if I might prevail upon you, what about as an idea?

**Pat.**    You've lost me again.

**Q**    What about the provenance of the idea that inspired it?

**Pat.**    If you're asking me where do the ideas come from…

**Q**    Exactly.  What lies behind them?  What is there in *their* background?

**Pat.**    [Shouting] **Nothing**!

**Q**    Oh!  Is that a sensitive topic?

**Pat.**    This talk about backgrounds.

**Q**    Why, I wonder, are you suddenly so touchy?

**Pat.**    *I* wonder if you wouldn't be touchy, subjected to such an inquisition.

**Q**    Inquisition?  Do you feel you are being tortured?

**Pat.**    I'm feeling you want me either to confess or to denounce something.

**Q**     And what might that be?

**Pat.**  You don't catch me like that.

**Q**     Ha!  That very admission springs the trap, does it not?

**Pat.**  I want to leave.

**Q**     How can you leave – now?

**Pat.**  I came here willingly and I have the right to leave as I will.

**Q**     Are you really that innocent?

**Pat.**  There is no reason for me to kept here against my will.

**Q**     That's no longer your decision. Look at this:  what does <u>this</u> mean?

**Pat.**  It's simply the title.

**Q**     But is it simply the title? Is it even a title?

**Pat.**  It's what I chose to give it.

**Q**     Why that?  Why NG959505?  Why not NG959*4*05?

**Pat.**  I'd already used that.

**Q**     Let me see … so you had.  Here it is.  They are very similar are they not?

**Pat.**  *It's how I work.*

**Q**     Indeed.  Here, a little earlier, I find NG9*58*505. What, I wonder, is that telling me?

**Pat.**  *They are simply identifiers.  It's how I choose to distinguish them.*

**Q**     And perhaps, might I suggest, to recall if not, indeed ….. to re-live?

**Pat.**  *I'm not saying anything more.*

**Q**     You wouldn't care to tell me why you need to recall these places? For clearly, they are all places, are they not? These are not random numbers, are they? These are not the product of some idiosyncratic, cryptic coding system are they? No, the system itself isn't cryptic at all, but your use of it is, is it not? Except that we've been doing some …. digging and, if I might put it like this, matters are being exposed, exposing what it is that lies behind all of this. So now, perhaps, you'll oblige me with a little more divulgence, by being more forthcoming, by being more candid.

**Pat.**    *No! I can't! I mustn't! I* …. don't talk about … it!

*I…. don't talk about … it!*

## XXIV

# SAINT VALENTINE'S DAY

It was February 13th. We had transferred to the library. There, surrounded by old walls made invisible by seamless bibliothèques, coffee and decanters awaited – as did a man who had not dined with us. Supper had not been formal; there were no dinner jackets; yet the unknown, elderly man was clad entirely in black.

'You'll forgive me, I'm sure' said our host 'if I leave introductions until later. Let me just say, for the time being, that this gentleman is part of my contribution to this evening's literary proceedings'. The gentleman in question nodded gravely at the inquiring faces and raised a silent glass in courteous salute.

We were a mildly assorted group, but with a common interest and none who could be said to be "fresh out of the nursery". Every month we met (in the reading room of the town's fine Carnegie library) to share what we had written: every month a different title and every month an assortment of valiant verse and compressed prose. Annually, however, our patron would invite us all to dinner and then to share our latest endeavours in superior comfort confined by his own towering shelves. So there we all were, ranged about a fine log fire, juggling with cups, glasses and texts, intrigued by the *inconnu* whose gaunt face, to me at least, seemed vaguely familiar, though I could not think why.

'As host it falls to me to start our proceedings and then we'll go clockwise so as to end with our guest. So, for this month's title, "Saint Valentine's Day", I give you this haiku:

> *Scented envelope*
> *Palpitating paper-knife.*
> *Vex'd expectations.*

The five-year stint in Tokyo, his final and most prestigious posting, had left a deep impression on Sir Francis.

And so the baton, as it were, was passed around our little group. By chance, three of us had concentrated on the name Valentine itself (or its variants) rather than on its commercial or romantic aspects. Elaine, a retired architect, recounted a droll and not altogether flattering tale about one of her former lecturers. He, Valentino Commorro, younger brother of the once-fêted painter Edouardo Commorro and to whose influence he owed his job rather than to any architectural or pedagogic ability, was distinguished solely by his car (a vintage 1934 V12 Packard roadster); his penchant for wide-brimmed fedoras, emulating Bugsy Siegel, Lucky Luciano, Humphrey Bogart and, of course, Al Capone; and his habit of leaning against corridor walls for never less than an hour at a time debating some trivial issue, always to arrive back where he'd started completely unswayed by any other opinion. His infamous dismissal of a student's design with the words "Have you ever seen it done like that before? No? Well, the chances are it can't be done" neatly encapsulated his idea of encouragement.

I, in my turn, read a story I'd devised about the extravagantly named Anna Jeanne Valentine Marianne Glans de Cessiat-Vercell who, fortunately for posterity, chose to call herself more simply Valentine de Saint-Point. (Saint-Point was where her famous great-uncle, Alphonse de Lamartine, had lived.) Valentine's story was poignant. Born in 1875 into a bourgeois Lyonnais family, she herself was variously poet, painter, playwright, art critic, choreographer, lecturer and journalist. Two manifestos are her most enduring legacy, particularly the second, *Manifesto Futurista della Lussuria*, i.e. a Futurist Manifesto for Lust – together with what she termed *La Métachorie*, proposed as a "total fusion of all arts" – in fact a highly personal form of expressive dancing that prefigured Isadora Duncan's. Her circle included famous artists, writers, politicians, musicians and she died a starving, raddled pauper in a back-court Cairo brothel.

We had gone almost full circle. Sir Francis stood again and with an expansive gesture announced

'And now, let me introduce someone who really should, as they say, need no introduction since I'm sure most of you will have encountered him before – not, perhaps, in person but nevertheless in your sitting rooms if your wirelesses were ever tuned into *The Mask of Dread*. Of course! That was it! The man dressed all in black, sitting in the shadow of an Orkney chair, was none other than The Man in Black himself, the actor whose weekly episodes of *The Mask of Dread* had kept my younger self glued to my parents' wireless set for half an hour each week as he narrated another of John Carse Dixon's mysteries. And I'd seen him before – not as The Man in Black but as the sinister Dr Murdo Moraine in the film *Only Owls To Go* based on a Margery Allingham story. When he spoke, it was with the sepulchral, clipped voice that I remembered. His name was Valentine Doyle. This, though, was a very much older Valentine Doyle.

'Thank you, Sir Francis. Good evening. I have a short tale that I hope will intrigue you, a tale which, like others you have already heard this evening, concerns a Valentine, not myself nor one of the thin cardboard variety, but of the living kind – initially, at least. She was called, in the theatre, on the billboards and in the pages of *Film Weekly, Picture Show, The Stage, La Petite Illustration* and *Varietà* as Vittoria Polenta; but her real name was Valentina Beatrice Carello di Fieno'. He paused to take a sip from his glass as I realised that the woman he was taking about was my grandmother – not that he could have known that. As for me, I had never connected my grandmother with Vittoria Polenta. To me, all those years ago, she had been an affectionate old lady in an apron both flowery and floury who could clasp a Hovis loaf to her bosom and saw off perfect slices of incredible thinness. The very occasional allusion to a thespian past seemed always to be hushed as if smacking of decadence or immorality.

So, though I was dimly aware of there being such a past, I had assumed it to be something essentially amateur or, at least, no better than end-of-pier reviews, pierrot troupes or concert parties. As for her having an Italian name: that is equally true of thousands of Scots. But could my own, late grandmother really have been a once-celebrated actress known as Vittoria Polenta?

Doyle extracted from a deep pocket a faded, decayed sepia photograph and passed it round for inspection.

'That is she. That is, or was, Vittoria Polenta'. Two large dark eyes in islands of kohl beneath heavily made-up eyelids and dark eyebrows stared coyly at the camera. A wide, sensual mouth, smiled faintly above a strong jaw, slightly cleft; from a clear centre parting, two immense, dark, slightly wavy tresses framed her cheeks and cascaded to her waist, artfully concealing her otherwise unconcealed bosom. It was not the kind of image one would expect of one's grandmother and certainly not one I'd ever seen. But it was undoubtedly she.

'That' continued Mr Doyle 'was Valentina Beatrice Carello di Fieno, a.k.a. Vittoria Polenta, on the set of a silent movie *Lucrezia Borgia* in which she played the eponymous lead. She was not yet twenty – and never would be. She disappeared while swimming in the sea, lost and therefore presumed drowned; the film was never completed. The feverish film industry went into extravagant mourning; the magazines I've mentioned ran maudlin obituaries; and in her tiny, hill-top home-town of Novara di Sicilia there was a commemorative mass said

*Vittoria Polenta*

in Santa Maria Assunta, the town's modest duomo, followed by a funeral procession behind an ancient horse-drawn ancient hearse bearing a vacant coffin'.

I was confused. What Doyle was saying was surely nonsense. Interruption would be discourteous; patience might bring clarity; and, if not, there would likely be a chance later to talk about it. Mr Doyle, Valentine Doyle, having further diminished the contents of his glass, continued....

'That, you might think, would have been the end of it. A young, beautiful, promising actress lost to the Mediterranean waves; the mournful process of remembrance in the steep streets of Novara di Sicilia and in the incense-heavy, marble arcades with their gilded Corinthian capitals of its shrunken cathedral. Until, several months later, the seasonal tunny fishermen (the

*194*

*tonnari*) of Scopello away to the north-west of the island, enacted their brutal, annual *mattanza*. Vast nets are drawn ever more tightly round whole schools of tunny so as to foment a foaming, threshing cauldron where those huge fish are then harpooned at close range by dozens of men standing in the broad-beamed, flat-bottomed boats that together form a maritime prison yard, termed *la camera della morte*, where they are finally clubbed to death. It is bloody; it is crude; it glorifies slaughter; it is a machismo bonding ritual; it is the event that, by chance, also delivered the mutilated torso of a young woman who, the *carabinieri* decided, had once been Vittoria Polenta. A month later World War I overtook that gruesome carnival and Vittoria Polenta was largely forgotten. In Novara di Sicilia a certain coffin was exhumed, augmented and hurriedly re-interred, without ceremony. But, for me, having come across this sad sequence quite by accident, it could not be the end of the story, despite the shadowy, second sepulture. There were too many unanswered questions: questions remaining now and certainly questions then, but of which there is no record. It intrigued me; it fascinated me; it grew to be an obsession. Why should this be? I cannot say. Was it only that I and Valentina Beatrice Carello di Fieno share, partly, a name? Was it simply one actor, acknowledging more than his fair share of success and the guilt that that brings, attempting to assuage his unease by an act of – what? Pity? Piety? Remembrance? I don't know: but, with time on my hands and, perhaps, an irrational instinct, I did my best to part the curtains of the past and investigate the circumstances of Valentina's death: the details of her film contract; the studio's finances; her connections with Novara di Sicilia and certain local groups; the rumours of her affair with the much older director and actor Ignazio Lupi; and more. There were curious inconsistencies, contradictions, anomalies which, eventually, took me from Sicily to London and the National Records Office: particularly what are termed the "Incoming Passenger Lists" '. He paused and took another sip.

My pulse was quickening. It hardly seemed possible that here, in this old house barely two miles from a small, ancient Scottish burgh I should, under the most improbable circumstances, learn something utterly unexpected about my own grandmother. I was shaking. So too, I noticed, was Valentine Doyle. Then, with no other warning, he slumped to the floor. One of our group, Dr Laurie, sprang to the sprawled figure. Somewhere a clock was striking midnight. She felt for a pulse; she felt for a heartbeat; then looked up at us and said ruefully

'In one way, I fear this ain't Valentine's day'.

## XXV

# NO MORE

Rain falls vertically, relentlessly, as it has for days, as it has for nights. There's but slight difference between days and nights. Days are perhaps a little lighter, but such light comes not so much from the sky as from the street-lamps bleary in the driving fog, ever reflected in the scudding puddles driven oppugnantly across the patchy tarmac, eddying and crashing against the far kerb. The bar's illuminated sign spits and flickers, its krypton tube italicising the bar's incongruous name. It does little to alleviate the murk, its inverted reflection shredding and shimmying with the wind-lashed pools below – where the dogs drink. The pack – some five or six, all large and of indefinable lineage – has roamed the town for days, scavenging, brawling, suddenly running for reasons unknown and, just as suddenly, stopping as if to confer – merely by means of glowering, mutual suspicion. He watches as one rummages in the shallow recess that surrounds the bar doors – a cheap, flush pair in need of paint, each with a single glazed panel, and apostrophised by flanking, naked, neon tubes, fixed upright. He has been watching from a close opposite for nearly two hours, coat collar turned up, bare-headed, scarcely sheltered by the close's iron lattice. In all that time no-one has left the bar; no-one has entered. His breath escapes like smoke into the saturated air; perhaps he is smoking – it's hard to tell. The shoulders of his coat are dismal with damp and his hair, patchy, alopœcic, is plastered to his scalp.

An elderly Moskvitch sluices to a halt opposite. Its driver runs for the cover of the bar whose doors are briefly pushed open to reveal a bare, tiled passageway and the top of a timber stair-way. His coat is long and leather. Her husband. He waits five minutes more and then leaves his foxhole to splash across. A dog half turns and bares its teeth half-heartedly, its coat matted and sodden, its tail low, its ears likewise, before it slopes off, scowling over its shoulder.

He is mugged by the heat and the smoke. He stands for a minute dripping on to the tiles, feet soaked from fording the street; then they squelch on the steps as he begins the descent to the bar, skirting crates of empty bottles stacked all the way up the centre of the square stairwell. At the cloakroom counter the woman regards him with weary concern as she transfers his wet macintosh to a hanger on the rail behind her. She is probably just old enough to be his mother; it's difficult to tell since he is wearing badly and she rather well. But her attitude, if not maternal, would befit an aunt.

'You should go home – you know that. She's a witch – and I've told you that before'. She flicks her cigarette into the large plate before her, and watches pityingly as he ignores her warning and heads for the flight down to the bar itself. She has not mentioned the woman's husband.

The tables are but sparsely taken. At perhaps no more than half of them someone sits, mostly alone, some in uniform; one or two still wear their officers' peaked caps. In the near darkness, faces are hard to make out. Conversation is dull. A harmonium-player, somewhere, is playing a mesmeric phrase, over and over again, its repetition like acoustic wallpaper, its pattern creating an insistent sound-screen expanding in all directions. His table, the one he prefers, is half-hidden by a concrete column, but from it he can still see the stage; and the waiter knows where to find him. The first *pálinka* arrives unbidden. So does the man in the long leather coat. He sits, uninvited, blocking the view. He smiles engagingly, with his teeth, stares quizzically, nods. The man lets the harmonium-player's Leitmotiv do the talking, as if making the same point incessantly. Eventually, getting no reaction, he says

'You should go home – you know that? She's my wife – as I've told you before. If I find that you have …. messed with her, you can expect a broken neck …. though not necessarily your own'. He stands and, with a mocking caress, fades back into the darkness.

On the stage a man with a grotesquely deformed right hand is nevertheless playing a small, two-octave piano-accordion. The rhythm has changed to that of a very slow tango, no more than sixty beats per minute, *1*-2-3-4, *1*-2-3-4, *1*-2-3-4, *1*-2-3-4, those same four bars are repeated and repeated and repeated – a new Leitmotiv. An alto-saxophone is providing discreet accents, but it's still the same phrase, still the same Leitmotiv. The harmonium-player has also adapted. In the dark a spot-light finds her, just. She is leaning against a steel stanchion, microphone enfolded by her right hand, her left hand both stroking her long hair and holding a cigarette, smouldering upright. Her eyes are closed. Her voice is low, barely singing – words spoken as much as sung. Her black, p.v.c. jacket reflects such little light as there is in shifting patches; the neck is turned up. She is smiling quietly to herself, inwardly, as though musing aloud, barely aloud, whispering, sometimes no more than a

Her eyes were closed

c r o a k ,  w o r d s punctuated by long pauses.

*It's all over*
*It's all done*
*It's all past*
*It's all gone*
*Can't be good*
*Not any more*
*Any more … (perhaps)*
*Never more.*
*Start again?*
*I'm afeart*
*I'm nae shuir*
*I've nae hert*

She lets the saxophone and harmonium ruminate sadly on those essential four bars, returning again and again to where they began.  She continues to stroke her hair, staring unseeing into the gloom about her. Who is she addressing? Herself? Or is it him? Maybe her husband. He stares sightless into his empty glass.  Twenty-four bars elapse before she speaks again (and her words are at first spoken rather than sung yet still keeping to the slow tango rhythm); they are confidential, intimate.  But talking to whom?

> *It's what you've got / that you should love ~*
> *at present, now, / what's more to get?*
> *Your pledges though / stick in your throat.*
> *I'll not allow / I will not let ~*
> *you go… / you shan't be free.*
> *I will bind you / chain you down:*
> *I've got the strength / I'd see you drown ~*
> *to keep you here / here with me.*

As a reflective aside she adds

> *Resolution?/ That is mine,*
> *knowing with him, / everything is fine.*
> *But separated / life's  a pain*
> *you do not need / birdbrain!*

There is a long brooding interlude; even the musicians seem deep in thought until she comes to herself again and begins to croon huskily, meditatively, confused, at times self-mocking:

*That would be that / over, clever.*
*But is it ever? / Is it ever?*
*Never's such a long time / at the going rate.*
*So oblivion could be / worth the wait.*
*The Nirvana Bar/ sells "Heaven's Star"*
*That might be better / best by far.*
*Love? / Whatever 'tis you've got?*
*Done it, done /…. it's not.*
*It's over / who's to know?*
*He couldn't leave / he wouldn't go.*
*He's never gone / Maybe, maybe so.*
*Maybe ……./ Never.*

The hypnotic rhythm drives on, but the spot is cut and she is engulfed in shadow, a departed soul. The light has gone out on the torch-singer.

The station is all but abandoned. Trains still call, though few. The main building, once quite smart, is decayed, its corrugated iron roof rusty, no longer intact; the harling now patchy and scabbed, the painted embellishments all defaced. The arched, ground-floor windows are all boarded up; those on the upper floor mostly broken. Damp defiles the roughcast plinth. A tree squirms out of the foundations. Outbuildings,

*The station is all but abandoned*

both brick and timber, are completely ruinous, roofs stripped of their tiles, rafters and trusses collapsed. The gravel bordering the single track is matted with grass, short now but rank in summer. Debris lies everywhere. On a siding, a forgotten carriage, largely stripped out, does duty as a waiting room, for those who risk its steps. Otherwise, shelter is where you can find it unless, like her, you have an umbrella.

It had shielded her well after she'd slipped out of the bar by its back stair, her knapsack stashed ready. She'd ignored the dogs and they her likewise. Now she waits in the lee of a wall straining to glimpse the headlight on the early-morning train limping towards its connection, eventually, with the fast train to

Budarestova. That's where she is heading. That's where she will be appreciated. In the capital there will be bars and clubs a-plenty that will give her work. It is done. It is over. He might not go, but she can. No more "maybes". No more "never". No more.

He knows exactly what she is thinking as, unseen but not unprepared, he watches her.

He, not only he, wants no more [30] [31].

# ACKNOWLEDGEMENTS

In the introduction to this collection I referred to the writing group that meets, not quite every month, here in my West Highland village. This entire, long-established, group has been a constant source of inspiration and motivation ever since I joined in November 2018. Titles for our monthly offerings of poetry and prose emerge almost accidentally in the course of informal banter, participants reacting instinctively to ideas generated in a flurried verbal tombola. While it can be invidious to single out particular members of any group, troupe or team: I feel I should thank two especially for their encouragement and support, namely Susanna Parochi and Carlos Escucha.

Note #30, below, acknowledges more fully my debt to Béla Tarr and Mihály Víg; and Egidia Neusman asks me to reiterate her debt to Sidney Paget as noted beside her illustration *Moncrieff Hames* on page 106.

Amandine Guise
Wester Ross
January 2020

# NOTES

[1]   *i.e. Sligo*

[2]   *pronounced "Geary".*

[3]   *absolutely exhausted ..... the majority of ferrets from F. to F. are infested with fleas.*

[4]   *As HMP Aberdeen was popularly known.*

[5]   *Oscar Wilde, "The Picture of Dorian Gray", ch. 11.*

[6]   *At that time Usmate was very small and had not yet been engulfed by Velate.*

[7]   *Dev'essere stata la tempesta.*

[8]   *Eventually, in the 1980s, Casa Borgia and its park became the property of the local Commune. The house and the gatehouse were both demolished, both being in a parlous condition. On the foundations of the central range rose a two-storey block of community offices, called Villa Borgia, in a simple, traditional Tuscan style. In 2007 a new civic library opened on the site of the former south wing; it too is in vaguely traditional Tuscan style, but has three stories. There is no sign of the gatehouse. That part of the gardens where I ate breakfast is now a public park; while the rest of the grounds is filled with private housing. The courtyard has been made into a very formal, paved area and is used for outdoor events, including theatre.*

[9]   *This story makes reference to several historical, Californian figures from the 1960s, including Allen Ginsberg, William Burroughs, Jack Kerouac and Dr Timothy Leary.*

[10]  *The Adventure of Black Peter* – Sir Arthur Conan Doyle.

[11]  *The Naval Treaty* – Sir Arthur Conan Doyle.

[12]  *A Case of Identity* – Sir Arthur Conan Doyle.

[13]  *The Testament of Gideon Mack* – James Robertson, Penguin Books, 2006.

[14] *Glossary, of Scots words:*

| | |
|---|---|
| *bygate* | side-road |
| *causeys* | paving stones, cobbles |
| *clart* | mud, muck |
| *courteours* | courtiers |
| *easins o' the sky* | horizon |
| *heugh* | crag, precipice, ravine |
| *mynd* | remember |
| *slauried* | besmeared |
| *stour* | dust, grit |
| *tae* | also |
| *trauchler* | one who trudges |
| *white-airn* | tin (i.e. the metal) |

[15] *The Taming of the Shrew, 2/i/340,* W. Shakespeare

[16] *The Tempest, 1/ii/402,* W. Shakespeare

[17] *Fleurs du Mal, Paysage,* C. Baudelaire

[18] *Elegy iv* (translation) E. M. Rilke

[19] *The Aberdeen Press & Journal*

[20] *Grid ref. NO 550639*

[21] *Grid ref. NO 548660*

[22] *I can find no direct attribution for this unusual place-name but suspect it's not unconnected with the Battle of Brechin (18 May 1452) in which the 4th Earl of Crawford (aka The Tiger Earl aka Earl Beardie) was defeated by the forces of the Royalist 1st Earl of Huntly following the defection during the battle by Crawford's entire left wing (consisting of the Angus bill-men) under the leadership of one Collace or Colossie, proprietor of Balnamoon.*
*See https://www.electricscotland.com/HISTORY/wars/24aBattleOfBrechin1451.pdf*

[23] *Battle of Mons Graupius*

[24] Battle of Stracathro 1130 when forces of David I under Edward Siwardsson slaughtered 4000 of the 5000 Moravian men for a loss of 1000

[25] 'I am the Tiger'. – Alexander Lindsay, 4th Earl of Crawford - see Note 22.

[26] James Carnegy-Arbuthnot, 6th Laird of Balnamoon – often described erroneously as "6th Earl".

[27] 'I don't understand'.

[28] The cabalistic numerical value of her name signifies "death``".

[29] Reference to Anselm Kiefer's "studio" near Barjac, Lozère.

[30] With acknowledgements and apologies to Béla Tarr and Mihály Víg whose film "Kárhozat" ("Damnation") with its song "Kész az Egész" ("Over and Done") performed by Vali Kerekes, inspired this story.

[31] There are several versions of the song, "Kész az Egész"; line order varies; in some cases lines are omitted; and translations show considerable differences. The song incorporated here is my own version based on several sources and then further modified to suit this story.

ISBN 9780953905799

00950 >